Summer of Wild Hearts

Angela Dorsey

Summer of
Wild Hearts

Typeset by Roberta L. Melzl
Editor: Bobbie Chase
Printed in Germany, 2010

ISBN: 978-1-934983-66-9

Stabenfeldt Inc.
225 Park Avenue South
New York, NY 10003
www.pony.us

Available exclusively through PONY.

Too long lonely
He wanders dark forests
Searching for family
To call his own

Loneliness stretches
Tramping wet meadows
Calling for others
Seeking for home

Desolate wanderer
Determined and headstrong
Hunting and hoping
Doomed to be alone?

Wake now!

Rusty's thought sliced through my dream like the sword I was holding – in my dream, of course. I'd been about to use it to stab the lock on the pirate's chest I'd dug up – again, in my dream. Even more exciting, I knew the chest contained my mom's secret, a secret that wasn't only in my dreams, unfortunately. Her mysterious past was all too real, all too irritating, and, no matter how hard I probed, all too unknown.

However, with Rusty, my wonderful gray gelding, mind-shouting in my head, the sword and chest and almost-revealed secret popped into oblivion. I opened my eyes to see early morning light creeping into my bedroom.

Intruder, thought Rusty, a little calmer now that he knew I was listening. His agitation felt like a million crickets shrilling all at once, and yes, in case you haven't guessed yet, I can feel horse thoughts and emotions. Especially Rusty's. He's the one who taught me how to use my gift – or my curse. I still haven't decided which it is.

Intruder? Who? I asked as I pulled on my jeans. My big toe caught in the hole in the knee and I lurched among my scattered clothes and books as I tried to free myself.

Rusty didn't waste time with words. He sent me an image: a muscular palomino stallion trotting across the unfenced part of our meadow, heading straight toward Rusty, Cocoa, and Twilight's pasture.

Finally into my jeans, I raced to my window. Yeah, there he was, all gold and ivory in the raw light, high-stepping toward our three horses and looking like one of my dreams turned real.

I reached out with my mind, careful to just listen and not speak. I could mind-talk to him, but I didn't want to risk scaring him. A bad experience in the past had taught me a horrifying lesson, and it had been a major relief to eventually find that the mustang I'd terrified with my mind-greeting had only been temporarily injured and not killed. But this is no time for side stories.

The palomino's intent told me he wasn't really trotting toward our *three* horses. He was trotting toward one and only one: Cocoa, my mom's chocolate brown mare. Uh-oh!

I switched my radar to Cocoa to find exactly what I'd expected. She was interested in him only because this was something new in her tame little world *and* she was

8

totally unaware of any danger whatsoever. She's kind
of clueless, to say the least. She wasn't even alarmed
enough to follow Rusty and Twilight, my almost-two-
year-old filly, as they did the smart thing and moved
away from the fence.

I didn't bother changing my pajama top for a T-shirt.
In seconds, the wild stallion would reach Cocoa and then
he'd try to break down the fence to steal her away.

"Mom!" I yelled as I crossed the living room section
of our small cabin. A muffled groan came from her
bedroom. "There's a wild stallion out here, trying to
steal Cocoa!"

"What?" She sounded all croaky. "What did you say,
Evy?"

I didn't bother answering. There was no time. One
of us had to get out there and frighten him off before he
damaged the fence or Cocoa or himself.

"Where's Loonie?"

Good question. Where was our ancient German
Shepherd? Why wasn't she barking? Didn't she see him?

My question was answered a moment later when I
almost tripped over her, curled up on the welcome mat
on the porch, fast asleep and snoring. I didn't bother
calling her to follow me. There was no point now. I'd do
her job for her.

I leapt down the stairs and ran toward the mustang,
waving my arms. The stallion was so focused on Cocoa
that he didn't see me. He was at the fence now, straining
into it and stretching over with his long, gleaming neck.

Cocoa stood two yards away, looking at him curiously as he snuffled to her. As I raced toward them, he reached even farther, his lips quivering just inches from her shoulder – and then his teeth snapped together.

His nip missed but obviously Cocoa didn't like his intentions. She laid her ears back and trotted snootily away. The stallion reared and an ear-splitting neigh rent the air, then he charged along the fence, fire flashing in his eyes as he followed Cocoa toward the barn. Toward me.

Closer. Closer.

"Hey!"

He didn't even hesitate. I waved my arms as he bore down on me.

"HEY!"

Shock reverberated through my body as he finally noticed the horrible human right in front of him. His panic made my own heart sound like a bass drum in my head. Then he spun away and sprinted for the protection of the trees, looking like a contender for the Kentucky Derby.

I watched him go with both relief and dismay. Relief, because both Cocoa and I were safe; me from being trampled and Cocoa from being abducted. And dismay for two reasons: first, he was simply gorgeous. I could've watched him prance about for hours. Second, his disappointment felt like someone jerking on a string looped through my heart. The poor guy thought he'd finally found a partner – until the loud, nasty human appeared from nowhere and ruined everything.

As he vanished into the forest, another of his thoughts struck me full force. He'd be back. He wasn't about to give up on the love of his life so easily.

Great. Now I'd have to start keeping Cocoa and Twilight in the barn at night. Cocoa wouldn't care too much, but Twilight? She was another matter. She wouldn't just hate being stuck in the barn. She'd loathe it. Detest it. Abhor it. The problem was that Twilight still didn't consider herself a domestic horse; she still felt like she was just hanging out with us for a while. If I forced her to sleep inside during the beautiful summer nights, she might decide to rejoin her wild herd.

Much belated, Loonie barked, then ranged around me to where the stallion had spun away. Her nose dropped to the ground and she sniffed fervently, her tail stretched straight behind her.

Cocoa wandered back to the fence and stared at the forest where the stallion had disappeared. Her huge groaning sigh gusted through the air. I reached out to touch her mind again. Bored. Like I needed to read her mind to know that. At least all the stallion had been was a diversion to her. Thank goodness. It would really be a tough situation if she wanted to be stolen away as much as he wanted to steal her.

"What's happening, Evy?" Mom called from the porch.

"There was a mustang stallion after Cocoa," I answered, walking back to the cabin.

"Is she okay?" Mom sounded ultra worried.

"Yeah, she's fine." Mom studied me like she was sure I was leaving out part of the story – and as you may have guessed, I was. She doesn't know about my ability to understand horses. No one does, except for one guy, Charlie, the Wild Horse Ranger, who guessed because of some Native American legend.

Not that I didn't *try* to tell her. I did, when I was little, and I'm still suffering from that single attempt. Whenever she notices anything about me that she thinks isn't 100% normal, she questions me and questions me. I don't see why she even worries – it's not like she's normal, with her hermit life and her mysterious past. I'd tell you more about that, but I can't. That's all I know, except that her self-induced exile to the wilderness has something to do with me. You'd think she'd tell me, since I have something to do with it, but nooo…

Mom yawned and headed back inside as Loonie trotted past me to the porch and wagged her tail at Mom beseechingly. Obviously the promise of breakfast meant more to her than the investigation of the mustang's presence.

A loud bawl erupted behind me. Tumpoo. He'd heard the commotion and wanted out of his stall now! Moose are so impatient. Tumpoo was only a few months old, but talk about demanding. You'd think he'd be a little more considerate since I saved his life last spring. I'd found him huddled beside his poor dead mother, and with Rusty and Twilight's help had brought him home. It took a long time and a lot of work, but eventually

13

Mom, my best friend, Kestrel, and I got him to eat. Now he eats constantly, getting bigger and stronger everyday – and lately he's decided that he's a comedian. I have to watch him every second or he'll play some practical joke, like climbing into the water trough and splashing the horses, or knocking over the woodpile, or tromping through Mom's vegetable garden, or chewing on the clean laundry hanging on the clothesline. It would be funny, except who has to clean up after him and fix all the things he destroys? You guessed it. *Me*.

Hoping to save myself later chores, I detoured into the barn and got Tumpoo's cracked corn ready, then put it outside in front of the barn doors, all to the beat of Tumpoo drumming on his enclosure. I hurried back to open his door before he could hurt himself or his stall, and a brown whirlwind shoved past me. He raced for the corn and dove headfirst into his breakfast, not looking up until he'd swallowed at least four times. You'd think I was starving him or something.

I meandered over to him and patted his glossy coat. Even though he was a pest, I was proud of him. He was healthy and happy, and was only just starting to get aggressive, which is actually normal for moose. They have to be belligerent to survive in this hard country, and Tumpoo was going to be one great survivor. His front-legged strike was already formidable. Plato and Socrates, our black and white barn cats with mismatched blue and green eyes, scrambled to high ground whenever they saw him now.

"Good boy, Tumpoo," I murmured. He narrowed his eyes at me as if I was threatening to eat his corn. "We'll go get you some fresh sticks today and try again with the moose food, okay?" His heap of willow twigs – normal moose fare – was drying up and becoming unpalatable. Not that I had any hope he'd eat them if they were fresh. Basically, I was a failure as a moose mother; I couldn't even teach my baby how to eat the right stuff.

"Evy! Breakfast!"

I gave Tumpoo a final pat and looked back at the horses. They were grazing serenely. My work here was done, at least for a while. "Stay out of trouble," I said to Tumpoo and then hurried toward the cabin.

Mom didn't waste any time. "We have to start keeping the mares in the barn at night," she said as soon as I walked inside.

I kept my mouth shut, not because I don't like a good argument, but because there was only one thing to add to the discussion and I didn't want to bring it up: Loonie. She used to be good at keeping wild animals away, but for the last couple of months she'd been failing in her guard dog duties. It was like she didn't hear intruders. And sometimes, if I was far away, she didn't even hear me. But I couldn't bear to talk about how my oldest friend might be going deaf.

As if she expected me to argue about Twilight, Mom continued, "She stayed inside at night during the winter. This is no different from then."

"It's totally different. Daylight that lasts until late and

15

starts again three or four hours later would make any horse hate to be inside, except maybe Cocoa," I argued, but with a tone so mellow and conversational that Mom looked over at me with surprise. She flipped a fresh pancake out of the pan and onto a plate, then handed me the plate. My stomach rumbled as I sat at the table. "Thanks, Mom. It smells awesome."

She waited, hands on hips, for me to say more, but I just cut my pancake into square bites. How could I add that my beloved dog was getting old? It felt too awful to even think about. And besides, I wondered if Mom had had the same unwelcome realization about Loonie that I had, and the same wish that it wasn't true. Why else would she stop complaining about the deer and rabbit damage done to her vegetable garden?

A loud thud made me jump and syrup splattered across the table. The bang came again and this time I noticed the front door shaking.

"Tumpoo," I had time to say before Mom rushed past me with the broom in her hands. She flung the door open and shoved the straw end toward Tumpoo's nose. The poor calf's eyes almost popped out of his head as he leapt back to avoid the whirling dervish that was my mother. His legs tangled together, but somehow he made it down the stairs, and then he collected himself enough that he could gallop toward the barn in that ungainly, hilarious way that moose run.

Mom shut the door quietly and hurried back to the kitchen area, as if ashamed of her outburst. I kept a straight face as I concentrated on my food, but I couldn't stop from laughing on the inside – until I thought of my homework, that is. I was getting behind again on my home schooling, and I'd promised Mom yesterday that I'd finish my latest assignment *before* Kestrel arrived today. Her once-a-week visit in the summer months is a big deal, because no one else ever comes to visit us. Okay, not quite true. Edward, Mom's agent, comes two times a year. And Kestrel's parents show up every month or so. And Charlie, the Wild Horse Ranger I mentioned earlier, drops in whenever he's in the area. But seriously, that's it. Ever.

I'd just put the first heavenly bite of apple cinnamon pancakes with butter and maple syrup into my mouth, when the all-too-familiar rumbling came from outside. The avalanche continued for fifteen long seconds, which was just long enough for all the wood to tumble from the woodpile.

"You better go see if he's okay," Mom said, her voice resigned.

I didn't feel nearly so resigned as I stomped toward the door. It was the second time this week that Tumpoo had knocked over the woodpile! My muscles were just starting to recover from the last time I'd picked up and stacked the two cords of wood. That moose better be long gone by the time I got out there. I even thought of grabbing Mom's broom.

Tumpoo wasn't gone. He was actually wading into the thickest of the firewood, sniffing and nibbling bark here and there. And he wasn't alone. He had two accomplices: Loonie, who was watching, and Twilight, who was *leading* the way into the jumble of wood. The second Loonie saw me, a guilty look flashed into her honey-brown eyes and she started to bark at the two scoundrels.

"Give it a rest, Loonie," I said – a little harshly, I admit. I was just ticked that she didn't bark at Tumpoo and his partner-in-crime before they tumbled the pile.

How did you get out? I mind-asked Twilight, irritably.

A wave of amusement washed over me as she turned to face me, her eyes bright with humor.

Not funny! I stomped my foot to further make my point. *I have to fix. No ride until I fix.*

This sobered her immediately. She pinned her ears and bit Tumpoo lightly on the top of his neck. *His fault.*

You should have stopped him.

She just snorted at me, shook her mane, then picked her way out of the jumble. Obviously, she didn't want to talk to me anymore. I watched her trot toward the barn, Tumpoo bawling and kicking as he hurried after her. She looked back and slowed at one point, giving him a chance to catch up. Brat One and Brat Two were becoming friends – great. My work would *never* be done now.

I looked for Loonie, thinking she'd stay to keep me company as I cleaned up their mischief, but no, she was gone. I kicked a log, and then hopped around a bit, holding my foot. The pain faded little by little, and when I could finally think of something other than my

foot, I sat on the chopping block, leaned my chin on my fists, and stared at the jumble of wood. With Tumpoo's moose behavior – which he couldn't help – and Loonie's age – which she couldn't help either – combined with Twilight's odd sense of humor – which she could totally control if she wanted – I was close to the end of my rope. At that moment, I never wanted to see their cute little animal faces again.

"Honey, come inside and finish eating." Mom's voice came through the window. "I'll help you clean up."

My frustration released in a rush of air. At least someone cared and understood. Well, Rusty understood and cared too, but he didn't have any hands to help me pick up wood.

Remembering Mom and Rusty's support, I felt a bit better – but only a bit. I needed to fix this situation, which meant figuring out some way to train Twilight and even Tumpoo, a wild moose. It seemed impossible.

But not as impossible as figuring out some way to help Loonie. Old was just old. Deaf was just deaf. There was no way to fix that.

Kestrel arrived just as we were finishing. She dismounted her old bay mare, Twitchy, tied her to the porch, and helped us with the last chunks of wood. When we were done, I asked Mom if I could put off my homework until that evening and Kestrel immediately said she'd help me.

Mom agreed, a little too eagerly. She knew we wanted to get out for a ride, and I'm guessing she wanted some peace and quiet for herself, too. She'd been working on a new painting, one of Tumpoo trying to graze. Yes, you're right, moose don't graze. But Tumpoo doesn't know that. His legs are way too long and so he has to keep them sprawled wide, plus bend them at a weird angle. Mom, of course, was painting him to perfection. I wondered what her agent, Edward, was going to think about this one. She'd recently switched from landscapes to mustangs, which he hadn't seemed too thrilled about. And now comedic moose? He'd probably have a fit.

Mom told us to either take Tumpoo with us or put him in his stall, and as we walked out to the pasture to get Rusty, I had every intention of taking him with us – until I found the water trough tipped over.

"Do you want me to help you fill it again?" Kestrel asked, sounding completely unenthusiastic.

"No. I can do it when we get back. I want to get out of here."

"Won't Cocoa and Tumpoo get thirsty?"

"They have water in their stalls, so Cocoa will be fine. Tumpoo will be okay for about ten minutes, which is how long it'll take him to splash it all over."

"He's kind of a brat, isn't he?" Understatement of the year.

I laughed – not a ha-ha-funny laugh, but the I'm-growing-bitter kind. "Know what scares me? What's he going to be like when he gets older and bigger and smarter?"

"Well, where do you want to ride today?" Kestrel asked, wisely changing the topic.

We discussed it as I lured Tumpoo into his stall with some corn and hay, plus some of the twigs, in case he decided to eat like a moose. He didn't seem to mind as we rode out of the yard, or I heard no heartbroken calls anyway. I guess he was ready for a rest after his morning of mischief making.

Twilight, however, wasn't remotely tired. She danced and leapt around us as Rusty and Twitchy carried us sedately away from the cabin.

Eventually, we decided to go to Cartop Meadow, where I'd seen mustangs in the past. If we were lucky, they'd be there, waiting to be quietly watched – another good reason to leave our naughty moose behind. Maybe we'd be really lucky and get to see Twilight's old herd. She'd love that.

As we rode, I caught Kestrel up on our news, which mainly consisted of seeing the mustang stallion. I was sick of talking about Tumpoo's pranks. I told her about the stallion focusing on Cocoa and how I was afraid he'd come back. She asked all the right questions and made all the right comments, but something was missing. She seemed distracted and kept staring off into the distance with a frown on her face. When I finished my spiel by saying I didn't know what to do, there was silence. She didn't offer her usual solutions to my problems. Something had to be wrong.

"So what's happening at your house?" I asked.

"Nothing."

Yeah, right. Like I believed that. "Well, something's different. I'm not stupid, you know."

"What do you mean, *different*?"

"You know what I mean. Your body's here, but your brain's in fantasyland."

"I was just thinking, that's all."

"Exactly. Thinking about what?"

"Well…"

I waited for her to continue. She didn't. "Well?" I prompted.

Kestrel sighed, finally accepting that I wasn't going to let her get away with saying nothing. "I wasn't going to tell you until after I decided."

"Decided what?"

"I've been thinking about going away to school next year."

"What?" My entire body went cold. Kestrel couldn't leave. She was my best human friend, my *only* human friend. I swallowed my fear so I could squeeze another word out between my clenched teeth. "Where?"

"A boarding school in Vancouver. It's supposed to be really cool, and I'd get real teachers instead of just Mom and Dad. I'd get to go on field trips, see movies, go shopping, and all sorts of things."

"But, but… " But what could I say? It would be awesome – for *her* anyway.

"Except I'd miss it here. I'd be gone until next June, not counting Christmas vacation, and you'd probably have a whole bunch of adventures without me." She sighed again. "But going away could be good too. I don't know what to do."

And I didn't know what to say. Of course she'd have fun, plus she'd get to do all sorts of things that we *never* do here, *normal things* like watch TV and hang out with friends and go to the mall. Even though I've never seen a mall, I imagine they're fantastic with lights and colors and noise and people, people, people everywhere.

But she was right about missing out, too. She'd miss visiting me, or at least I hoped she'd miss visiting me.

Okay, but who was I kidding? My entourage of pesky animals and I don't compare to movies and parties and tons of friends.

Leaving: one point. Staying: a big fat zero.

The education would be better. Leaving: two points.

The seeing-more-of-the world factor was infinitely better. Three points.

And the mentioned adventures? Adventures could be had anywhere. They'd just be a different kind, that's all.

Since pros and cons weren't going to back me up, I resorted to whining. "If you leave, it will be so awful here. I'll be stuck hanging out with Mom all the time."

"I'd really miss you too."

"But you'll make new friends."

"I'll still miss you. We'll always be best friends. And I'll miss the animals."

The animals. So I wouldn't be left totally alone. I'd have my trusted Rusty, my sweet Loonie, my free-spirited Twilight, my irritating Tumpoo, and Cocoa, who liked me because I gave her oats and brushed her. What I wouldn't have was my best friend.

A new thought struck me like a slap. If Kestrel went, she'd change. I'd stay the same. When she came back next summer, she might not even *like* me anymore. I mean, why would she? I'm not remotely cool or anything.

Why sad? asked Rusty.

Talk later, I answered. I couldn't concentrate on two conversations at once, even when I wasn't saying much.

"Anyway, I haven't made up my mind yet," Kestrel said in the silence I'd let linger too long between us.

"When do you have to decide?"

"August 10th."

Less than one month.

For half a mile, all we heard was the thud of the horses' hooves, the birds singing, and the wind flipping the coin-sized leaves on the Aspen trees. Usually our silences were relaxed. Not this time. But how could I speak? My tongue was glued to the top of my mouth, and I knew if I tried to say anything, it would end up being the wrong thing, and then she'd leave for sure.

"There's one thing we can do to make sure we're together," Kestrel finally said.

"What?"

"You can ask your mom if you can come too."

A tiny hope sparked in my heart and quickly swelled. "That would be so..." Words failed me.

"Great? Fantastic? Amazing? Fun?" Kestrel suggested.

"All of the above." I laughed.

Kestrel's voice became cautious. "I just don't know how we can talk Laticia into letting you go. I know how much she, um, *likes* strangers."

"Or hates them, you mean." Reality bites. Mom would never let me go. She hates civilization and avoids other people as if they all carried the plague. Don't ask me why, though – she still hasn't told me, despite my best and sneakiest efforts.

"Hello!" A distant voice reached our ears.

We looked to our right to see a flash of red between the trees – Charlie, the Wild Horse Ranger, and his amazing horse, Redwing. We called hello back and turned our mounts to meet him.

Charlie tipped his cowboy hat at us when he rode up to us. "How are you ladies doing today?"

"Not bad," said Kestrel.

"How about you?" I asked.

Once the pleasantries were over, we got down to business. Charlie had heard about a mustang hanging around camps and trying to get friendly with the domestic horses. One man even had to shoot his rifle in the air before the wild horse was frightened off, and Charlie was worried about the horse's safety in case it approached the wrong people and was hurt or captured or worse.

I told him about the palomino who'd been at our cabin that morning, leaving unsaid that the stallion had almost trampled me and Charlie should be more worried about the people than the horse. I didn't say anything about the romantic feelings the mustang had toward Cocoa either. Charlie would understand how I knew since he knew about my "talent" but Kestrel still didn't know. I didn't want her thinking I was a freak – especially now that she might be meeting lots of normal, cool kids. We all concluded that it had to be the same horse, and moments later, Charlie and Redwing were loping back toward my place. Kestrel and I continued on toward Cartop Meadow.

As we rode, we talked about how fun it would be to go away to school together, but as the ground passed beneath our horses' hooves and Cartop came closer, I felt more and more miserable. I did my best to hide my feelings but I think Kestrel could tell how I felt. By the time we reached Cartop Meadow, we'd been riding in silence for about five minutes, and when we discovered the meadow was empty we turned around and rode back the way we'd come.

Twilight disappeared on one of her adventures for a while as we rode home – again, quietly. I tried to keep my mind open to what she might be doing, but I couldn't concentrate. This thing with Kestrel was grinding my peace of mind to bits.

If I asked Mom to let me go with Kestrel, she would say no and then I'd feel all mad and like I had to find some way to convince her. A massive task, judging from the secrets I'd been trying to wrestle from her for years.

And if I said nothing? If I didn't ask? Then Kestel would just go.

Sometimes, my life really sucked.

We were galloping across a meadow when I felt
Twilight's interest perk up. Though I couldn't see her,
she wasn't too far away and I could sense her emotions
easily. I tightened Rusty's reins a bit to slow him and
closed my eyes to concentrate on what she was feeling,
hearing, seeing.

Movement between tree trunks, she said, sensing my
question.

Twilight, come near. Safe with us.

Might be family.

I knew she'd hoped to see them at Cartop Meadow
and was disappointed when we didn't, but the chance of
the movement being one of her old herd was super low.
Might be danger.

If danger, will run, she thought to me, and stepped
forward.

I opened my eyes and pulled Rusty to a quick stop,
then turned him in Twilight's direction.

Twitchy's hoof beats slowed and stopped. "What's wrong?" Kestrel called back to me, sounding out of breath from our gallop. "What do you see?"

"Nothing, I hope."

Twilight, please come. My filly thought she was invincible. She thought nothing could outsmart her, catch her, or even *want* to harm her. I don't know where she got that last one from. What about the wolf that tried to eat her last winter, and the poachers that chased us just months ago? Why hadn't she learned from those experiences? She could be sneaking up on a bear right at that moment, and bears can run awfully fast if they don't have to run too far. Rusty moved nervously beneath me as he felt me think of bears. He knew enough to be cautious.

I heard Twitchy and Kestrel trot back to us and then...

A dark shape rushed toward me. Fear speared my heart and I leapt in the air. My legs felt a jumble as I tried to run away from the charging beast. It was gaining on me! Gaining! And then I caught my stride. As I darted nimbly through the trees and pulled away from it, my fear morphed to smugness, then to interest – my pursuer wasn't a bear. It was a horse.

As Twilight's fear lessened, I was able to grab it and wrestle it under my control. Terror free, for the moment anyway, I could think – and I could see what horse was after her.

My own fear spiked. The mustang stallion!

Run faster! I mind-yelled to her.

"Evy, are you okay?" I heard Kestrel ask, but her voice sounded from another world.

Steady, thought Rusty. *Gather yourself.*

Twilight didn't seem inclined to run faster. In fact, she was slowing down. She looked back as she loped along, checking him out. He looked terrifying to me – ears back, eyes hard, nostrils distended, muscles straining – but Twilight didn't seem to notice that.

"Evy?" Kestrel was sounding really worried now, but I didn't have time to answer her. I had to save Twilight. I understood what my young, inexperienced horse did not: she was in danger of being stolen away forever.

Run! Do not ask why. Run as fast as you can!

And for the first time ever, Twilight didn't question. She ran. I almost fell from Rusty's back in shock. Twilight had listened to me? Amazing!

Kestrel's hand gripped my shoulder. "Evy!"

With my filly racing through the forest toward us, trusting me enough that she ran even when she didn't feel danger, and with the palomino stallion pounding just yards behind her, fully intent on stealing her away from me, I turned to my best friend and tried to act as ordinary as possible. "Let's ride this way!" I said with artificial cheer – too loud, almost shrill. I smiled what I'm sure was a ghastly smile, then leaned over Rusty's neck and asked him to gallop toward the trees where Twilight would emerge.

If the stallion didn't catch her first.

"Evy? Evy, wait! Evy!"

"Twilight!" I yelled.

I felt the palomino stallion falter. He'd heard our shouting, and after his experience that morning with the freaky little human that appeared from nowhere, he was feeling a bit cautious. He slowed and stopped and sniffed the air, inhaling Twilight's scent. Memorizing it.

Twilight slowed to a lope when the stallion stopped chasing her and, moments later, trotted from the forest looking calm and serene. Her coat glittered in the summer sun and her blue-black mane shone like falling silk as she dropped her head to graze.

I, on the other hand, looked crazy.

I turned Rusty to find that Kestrel hadn't followed me on my mad dash toward the forest. She sat stock still on Twitchy in the center of the meadow, staring at me with a look that said she'd just realized I was completely and totally insane. Too soon, Rusty started walking back to Kestrel, and as we neared her, Twilight trotted past us, looking even more relaxed than before.

I stopped Rusty in front of Kestrel and swallowed nervously. "So I guess you want an explanation?" I asked in a small voice.

Kestrel nodded.

The problem was I didn't have one. If I told her Twilight had been in danger, she'd want to know how I knew, and I couldn't tell her about my gift, especially now. She'd never understand why I hadn't told her before, if she even believed me. There was a good chance she'd just continue to think I was nuts, and then she'd leave for boarding school *early* just to get away from me.

And I couldn't tell her a made up story, if I could even think of one in time, because Rusty hates lies with a passion and would probably toss me off his back.

If only Twilight had acted scared after she came out of the forest, or Kestrel had heard or seen the stallion, then I could tell her the simple truth – but all she'd seen was her best friend acting dazed and ignoring her, then yelling something ultra-stupid and galloping off…

Kestrel raised her eyebrows as she waited.

"Well, um, I thought Twilight was in danger." Lame, I know, but I didn't know what else to say.

Kestrel turned in her saddle to look at Twilight who, believe it or not, was now napping in the shade as she waited for us. "What made you think she was in danger?" she asked predictably. "She always takes off and comes back when she feels like it."

Adrenaline was still making me tremble, and my hand shook as I stroked Rusty's shoulder. "There was that stallion after Cocoa this morning and then when Charlie said there's a mustang causing problems, well…" Rusty humped his back and swished his tail. A warning not to stretch the truth too much. Kestrel watched me like she was still waiting for the crucial bit of information.

"I thought maybe the wild stallion was after Twilight,

trying to steal her." Might as well just state it outright. At least Rusty wouldn't throw me. "It was just a feeling. I can't say where I got the idea." All true.

"If that's what you really thought, I guess I can see why you'd act weird," Kestrel said, though she still looked perplexed.

"I wasn't acting *that* weird," I said. Even though Kestrel is obviously a forgiving sort, I still don't like it when she thinks I'm too strange. "If Twilight really was in danger, it would be perfectly normal to try to help her."

"I guess so," Kestrel agreed, too polite to argue with the lunatic. She knew as well as I that there was no reason, no clue, no indication of Twilight being in any danger whatsoever – but apparently, she'd decided to file this under *unexplainable*, along with all my strange actions of the past. Whew!

She turned Twitchy and we started riding side by side. Twilight got up and started dancing in front of us.

Stay near, I cautioned her.

She flipped her tail at me.

"Hey, do you think you'll be allowed to go to the rodeo this year?" asked Kestrel.

I reined in my Twilight annoyance before turning to Kestrel. "I doubt it, but I'm going to ask anyway, and probably be told *no,* just like every other year."

"Jon will be there," Kestrel teased.

"Why should I care?" I asked, even though the blood had rushed to my face. I met Jon a few months ago when a bunch of our neighbors dropped by unexpectedly to help my mom and me build an addition on our cabin. And I must admit, he seemed pretty nice.

"No reason." Blessed silence dropped between us, but only for a moment. "He's pretty cute, huh?"

"Really? I hadn't noticed." I stared straight ahead.

"Well, he thinks *you're* cute," Kestrel said, dropping her second biggest bomb of the day.

"How can you know that?" My voice felt all raspy.

"He told one of his friends, who told my sister, Nova, who says Jon must like you." Kestrel grinned, then laughed. "You're so funny, Evy. To most girls that would be a good thing, but you look like you just ate a bug."

"I do not." I tried to sound injured, but couldn't stop a small smile from creeping onto my face. "It's fine if Jon likes me. That doesn't mean I like him."

"Oh, okay," she said, sounding like she was trying to stop herself from laughing out loud.

What is wrong? asked Rusty.

Nothing. Nothing at all. The last thing I needed was for my horse to start teasing me about boys too. That would be too much. Thankfully, Twilight saved the day. In the same way she seemed to do everything – with bubbly recklessness. She pranced straight toward us, then reared away. Her hind legs propelled her forward like a bucking, kicking jet in the direction of the barn and cabin. I checked – yes, her mind was quiet. She just felt like being dramatic. Or maybe she sensed my discomfort and wanted to distract us from our conversation? Okay, so that's probably wishful thinking.

Beside me, Twitchy did a little hop. I looked at Kestrel, surprised. She was holding Twitchy's reins tight and the mare was actually trying to go fast. Amazing! Kestrel nodded and I smiled, then leaned over Rusty's back. Together we raced for home.

"We are *not* going to argue about this anymore. No rodeo means *no* rodeo!"

How infuriating could she be? How heartless and cruel and savagely malicious?

I slammed my foot down onto the floor exactly the way Twilight drove her hoof into the earth whenever she was mad – immature, I know, but I couldn't help myself.

Kestrel looked at me sideways, clearly embarrassed by our fight. I shook my head. I couldn't think of anything that would convince Mom to let me go. It was hopeless.

Kestrel looked pained when she saw the tears beading in my eyes, and she turned to Mom. "Evy will be with me the whole time," she said, though she had to know that Mom was going to keep saying no. But still I felt better. Kestrel had never joined our "discussions" before.

"I know that, Kestrel," Mom said, her voice much gentler than when she spoke to me. "But I won't be there to make sure she's safe. Your parents will be there for you."

"They won't mind if Evy's there too. They'll watch her." As if I was six years old or something, and needed a babysitter.

Mom shook her head. There was no hope. I turned and thundered off toward my room. For the first time ever, I wished my new room had a door to slam. The whisking sound of a curtain being thrown in front of the doorway just wasn't very satisfying.

"Why don't you come too?" I heard Kestrel ask from the other room, and strained to listen. I knew what she'd tell me if I asked her that question but maybe she'd be more honest with Kestrel.

Nope. She explained that she had work to do, that she couldn't afford the time off, that if she left this painting now it would be ruined. Excuses, excuses, and more excuses.

I flopped down on my bed and glared at the ceiling and wished I didn't have the self control to stop from screaming aloud. Why couldn't I go to the rodeo? I'd be perfectly safe with Kestrel and her family, and I was definitely old enough. All sorts of kids would be there, running around like packs of wild animals, and most would be a lot younger than me. Yet I couldn't go because of my hermit, scared-of-everything, paranoid mother.

"Evy?" Kestrel was outside my bedroom.

"Come in," I said, then quickly added, "Only you."

My door curtain moved and Kestrel's head came into

39

view. I motioned her the rest of the way, and she stepped quickly inside. The curtain fell back over the doorway as she moved to sit beside me on the bed. "It's not fair," she said quietly, so Mom couldn't hear us. "Laticia didn't even really listen to us."

"I know. She *never* does." Which wasn't quite true. She does listen sometimes. Just selectively. "But thanks for trying to get her to change her mind."

"If she won't even let you come to the rodeo," Kestrel added, despair in her voice, "she'll *never* let you come to boarding school with me."

"I know." I pressed my face into my pillow. What a horrible, stressful day. "I hate my life."

I felt Kestrel plop down on my bed, then a minute later, the bed moved again and I heard her unzip her backpack. "You have a letter from Ally," she said, in a fake upbeat voice. Positive, buoyant Kestrel was back.

"You don't need to try to cheer me up," I said, flinging my pillow across my room to rest beside my dirty clothes. "I'll get over it." Though I knew it would take a while – like twenty or thirty years.

"I brought you the latest horse magazine, too," Kestrel said, sounding even more ferociously cheerful. "There's a great article in there about ground tying."

"Rusty already does that. Do they have anything about mischievous moose calves?" I asked, still pretending that it didn't matter that my mother completely controlled my life.

Kestrel smiled.

"I guess we should let the little pest out of his stall. He's been in there for hours," I said, reluctantly. We'd have to walk past Mom to leave the cabin.

"He's going to be a little monster with all that saved up energy."

We paused at my doorway curtain, then I took a deep breath and led the way into the living room. Mom was in her painting corner, mixing colors. She looked up with a frown and I immediately averted my eyes. I didn't want to invite more discussion.

"Where are you going?"

"Barn," I said, because I couldn't say nothing. Then we were at the door.

"Don't leave without telling me."

I didn't answer. We shut the door behind us and ran toward the barn and pasture, and though I didn't look back, I could feel her eyes following us through the window.

Tumpoo started bellowing the moment we stepped inside the shady interior. He pressed against his stall door, his large, liquid eyes speaking piteously. I almost laughed at his show of sadness, despite my horrendous mood. When we opened the stall door, Tumpoo's false meekness disappeared in a flash, and as he darted past me I could see only trouble. "We'd better follow him," I said. "Maybe we can get him to burn off some energy down by the lake."

We gave the house a wide berth, cutting through the trees so Mom couldn't watch us through the window.

Tumpoo beat us to the lake and almost dove into the water. He was a true moose; he adored water.

Kestrel and I settled on the edge of the lake and watched him frolic. It was nice having a moose when he did normal moosey things. He was so cute, bobbing around out there, soaking himself with splashes, shaking the water off like a dog. He even lay down in the water for about half a second, leaping up when the spot he'd lain in was over his head. He still didn't like water in his face.

"I'm going to have to teach him how to eat the weeds under the water. Any ideas?" I asked Kestrel.

"Sticking your own head under?"

"I tried that," I admitted. "He looked at me like I was weird."

Tumpoo stopped near the willows and a dreamy look washed over his face as he mouthed the tender tips and picked at the leaves. I smiled for the first time since we'd gotten home. Maybe he was going to get this browsing thing after all, and on his own, too.

"I was just thinking, maybe we should work on Laticia like we do with young horses," Kestrel said, sounding so drowsy that I looked over at her. She was lying on her back, eyes closed, with the sun shining full on her face.

I did the same. It felt good, so bright behind my eyelids, so warm on my skin. I love summer. Tumpoo made gentle water sounds as he waded and munched, and the lapping and sloshing was soothing to hear.

"What do you mean?" I asked Kestrel, once I felt satisfactorily tranquil.

"Well, you know how it is with a young horse. You don't just throw a saddle on and ride it the first day. You start slow. Maybe she has to get used to you being gone just a bit at a time. You should start coming over to visit me more often."

"She's never let me before, for more than a couple hours, anyway."

"But we haven't asked for a long time. Maybe she'll let you come for an afternoon at first, and then maybe overnight. And then maybe for a couple of days for a special event, like when we do the branding, or whatever. Then, eventually, she might feel okay about you going to the rodeo."

"Yeah, next year. And the plan only works *if* you don't go away to school."

"Oh yeah." Silence.

Tumpoo splashed.

"But if you don't go," I said, trying hard to be positive, "it's a great idea."

"Maybe she'll even let us go visit Jon," Kestrel said, a teasing lilt in her voice.

I decided to ignore her little dig. "I just don't want to wait a whole year to go to the rodeo," I said.

"I know, that's really –"

Kestrel screamed as a shower of icy flecks cascaded over us. I didn't waste the energy screaming – I just leaped up and out of Tumpoo's shaking radius, which didn't make me move any faster than Kestrel, actually. I was just as wet and bedraggled as she was once we were safe from the flying mud and moose-water droplets.

"Gross!" Kestrel shrieked and tried to shake the mud from her sleeves.

I tried rubbing mine, thinking it might come off easier that way. Not! It just smeared dark along my sleeve. And then we were giggling and laughing, unable to stop, until our sides hurt and we thumped back to the ground, too weak to stand. Tumpoo tried to shake over us once more, but he was out of ammo, so he went back into the lake. After that, Kestrel and I took turns being the lookout while the other relaxed and enjoyed the sunshine. After a while he gave up and wandered back to the barn.

"Evy! Your homework!" Mom's shouted reminder floated toward us, barely audible.

I grimaced. Doing homework around Mom was going to be tough. I was still super angry at her, even though honestly, I don't like being mad. It makes me feel mean and grumpy and… well, mad.

As it turned out, it wasn't as bad as I thought it would be. With the curtain to the living room firmly closed, Kestrel and I whispered over my books for a while, then took a break while I read the pen pal letter out loud, and then we looked at the magazine that Kestrel had brought – with frequent glances out the window to see what Tumpoo was up to. Whenever he was out of sight, I'd ask Rusty if he could see the calf. Most of the time he could, and every time he updated me Tumpoo was doing something harmless. Maybe he was getting better. Maybe his *El-Destructo*, practical-joker stage was coming to an end. I could only hope.

Kestrel whispered half an article about a world-class three day event rider and her amazing horse, then handed the magazine to me so I could see the rider's picture before she turned the page…

"Oh, my gosh," I said, way too loud. I closed my flapping mouth.

"What is it?" asked Kestrel, snatching the magazine back.

I moved so we could look at the picture together. "Don't you see?" I pointed to the picture of the famous equestrienne, or rather to the wall behind her. "Morning Meadow."

"What?"

"That's Morning Meadow, one of Mom's paintings."

"Wow, cool! She's even more famous than I thought. This magazine goes all across Canada and the United States. Everyone's going to see that painting."

"That's awesome. Maybe people will start buying more of her paintings. Edward said they aren't selling."

"Isn't that weird? I mean, what are the chances of us seeing her painting in a magazine if not many are selling?"

"That is weird." I raised my eyebrows. "And it's funny that Edward didn't tell us that one sold to a famous person, too."

"Maybe she just bought it."

"Maybe, but they probably took this picture and

wrote this article months ago. I've heard that's how magazines do it. And Mom painted Morning Meadow almost a year ago."

"Maybe he didn't know she was famous," Kestrel said. Her face was perplexed, and I'm sure mine looked the same as we stared at the smiling equestrienne and Morning Meadow hanging stunningly behind her. "Are you going to tell your mom about it?" she asked.

I picked up my pen pal letter and waved it in front of Kestrel. "First, we ask Ally to help us. She lives in Vancouver, so she can go to Edward's gallery."

The next morning, after a big breakfast, Kestrel packed the letter we'd written to Ally with the rest of her stuff. I felt awful as I watched her get ready to go. She was only allowed over once a week, and if she went away to boarding school we only had four weeks left. Only four visits. And no rodeo together, either. Immediately, I was mad again.

"Can I go over to Kestrel's house for a little while?" The first words I'd spoken to Mom since last night.

"You can ride halfway with her. And you're lucky I'm letting you do that when you haven't finished your homework."

I didn't argue. Not because Mom was right – though I hadn't finished my homework, even after I promised her I would – but because I was afraid I'd yell at her again. Kestrel didn't need to hear us fighting anymore.

"Don't take too long," Mom added when I opened the front door.

I clamped my lips shut and plunged through the open doorway, leaving Kestrel to close the door behind us. I heard her start a polite thank you and goodbye to Mom, and then I was too far away to hear.

Inside the barn, I quickly opened Cocoa's stall door and the mare trotted out into the pasture. Twilight looked at me impatiently when I walked past her stall door without releasing her as well.

Want out!

Going for ride.

Twilight snorted softly. That was okay, then. She pulled another mouthful of hay from the manger and chewed methodically.

Tumpoo bawled for his breakfast. He wanted it *now,* so I got his corn ready as I waited for Kestrel. She showed up just as I was about to let the moose calf out. "I wouldn't stand between him and his corn, if I were you," I cautioned.

Kestrel moved to the side and I opened Tumpoo's door. He rushed past me, heading straight for his bucket.

Rusty waited for me at the pasture gate and minutes later we had him and Twitchy saddled. I turned Twilight loose to follow and we were off. It was a glorious morning for a ride, bright, clear, warm, and well, perfect. The robins were going nuts with all their singing, and loons wailed in the background. There was hardly a wisp of wind, only enough to tremble the rich green boughs.

"Isn't Tumpoo coming with us?"

I looked back. He was standing at the water trough,

splashing his belly with a front hoof. Soon he'd be inside the trough, and then for his final act he'd tip it and make mud from the water on the ground. I turned away. I needed a break from all things irksome – in other words, Mom and moose.

"He's having too much fun making more work for me," I said. "And I don't want him to catch up to us when he's finished making a mess. Let's hurry."

Because we hurried, the ride halfway to Kestrel's house was over long before I was ready to return home. Kestrel and I said a reluctant goodbye, then she disappeared around the corner.

I sighed, dismounted Rusty, and led him to the roadside to graze. Together, we meandered along the rough track as he clipped the fresh grass tips. Seeing that we were in dawdling mode, Twilight wandered ahead and lay down to nap as Rusty and I ambled toward her, slow as sun-baked turtles.

But still, even at our ultra pokey pace, we eventually came close to home – and the first thing I heard was Mom shouting.

What now? I wasn't even there for her to yell at.

But – uh oh – Tumpoo was.

Quickly, I climbed into Rusty's saddle and called Twilight, then we sprang into a lope, heading back to the never-ending trouble that was my life.

Trouble turned out to be more like a disaster. I got there just in time to see Tumpoo fling himself from the cabin, his ears flat back and his little cloven hooves flying. Mom was right behind him, wielding the broom like a sword and screaming, "Bad moose! Bad moose!" at the top of her lungs.

I pulled Rusty to a stop and for a moment considered turning him around and heading for the hills, but then Mom saw me.

"Do you know what he did?" she shrieked. My shock must have shown on my face because she collected herself somewhat and said in a slightly calmer voice, "He broke into the cabin when I was down refilling the horse's water trough." Tears studded her eyes. "You should see the mess he made."

I slid from Rusty's back.

Keep Tumpoo out of trouble? I asked Rusty.

Rusty snorted his assent and trotted off in search of the little brat.

I walked back to the cabin with Mom. "We have to do something, Evy," she said, still brandishing her broom.

"I know."

"He can't keep terrorizing us like this."

The damage he'd done to the cabin was amazing. First was the front door. Because it was a warm day, Mom had left the wooden door open and shut the screen door when she went to the barn. The screen hung in shreds where his sharp front hooves had sliced it into streamers. And that was just the beginning.

An ugly mess waited in the kitchen, where he must have been looking for treats. Flour spread across the floor, along with moose tracks and moose poop. The sugar bag had been sliced open by those same sharp hooves. The oatmeal was dumped and cans of soup and fruit and fish rolled about in the disgusting mixture. He'd even ripped one of the curtains in front of the cupboards.

Chairs were knocked over and the table was pushed up against the bookcase at the far wall of the dining area – which saved our books, thank goodness. But Tumpoo hadn't been finished yet. The floury tracks moved on. I followed them with a growing sense of dismay. He'd walked into Mom's room and jumped up on her bed, leaving behind dirty flour hoof marks. Her chair was knocked over – and on the other side of her room, so were her completed paintings! I felt my blood run cold, and for a moment, couldn't move.

In a slow motion nightmare, I walked toward the paintings. Bent. Picked them up, one by one. And was infinitely grateful each time that he hadn't perforated the painted canvas. They seemed damage-free except for a slight dusting of flour. He must have brushed up against them and knocked them over, that's all. What a relief!

I walked back into the living room/kitchen area to see no tracks leading into my room. He must have thought the curtain across my door was really a wall. Mom was standing in her work area by the front windows, her head in her hands. Her shoulders trembled. Oh, no. Had Tumpoo done something to one of her paintings there?

He had.

I could have cried.

Mom *was* crying.

What could I do but put my arm around her and lean into her side? "I'm so sorry, Mom," I whispered. My mom loves her paintings, which is probably why she's such a great artist. This one she'd finished last week, and it was a beauty too. In the foreground, a graceful red osier dogwood spiked the canvas, and behind the ruby stems, Rusty and Twilight stood like benevolent royalty watching the viewer. A steamy meadow spread behind them. The painting looked otherworldly and mystical, as if the viewer had chanced upon a concealed doorway to a secret world where horses reigned.

And in the bottom right corner? A neat rip the size of a small moose hoof.

"Come sit down," I said to Mom and led her to the big chair. She crumpled on the seat and stared out the window. Tears rolled down her cheeks and she kept her mouth firmly shut.

I sat on the arm of the chair beside her and rubbed her shoulder. "I'll figure out something, I promise."

She looked up at me with red eyes and nodded, too sad to even yell at me for bringing Tumpoo into our lives. I almost wished she would. Anger I could take, but sadness? Tears? That was the worst.

Trouble, thought Rusty.

"I'll be right back. I want to put him in his stall."

Mom didn't say anything as I left.

Of course, the water trough had been dumped again, already. Rusty was standing at the barn door, looking inside. I paused to thank him and give him a hug, then walked into the barn. Tumpoo was trying to climb the ladder into the loft, for a reason known only to himself. There was nothing up there but our two cats, Socrates and Plato – both of whom were staring down at Tumpoo and hissing. We hadn't bought our hay for the coming winter yet, and all the grain was in the tack/feed room. He'd probably tried that door first and found it too strong.

"Tumpoo!" I yelled, and the calf turned his head. Both hooves slipped on the ladder rung, one hoof toward the floor – and the other behind the rung. His leg squeezed between the ladder and the wall and slid down to the knee. I rushed forward. "Hold still, buddy," I said, trying to make my voice calm. If he struggled, he could so easily break that long spindly leg. I wanted our Tumpoo troubles to be over, but not that way.

Even as the blood pounded through my skull, even as my shaking hands took hold of his thin foreleg, even as I pulled his leg gently up and out from its prison, I marveled that he didn't struggle. He was frightened – I could see it in his eyes. But there was something else there too: complete and total trust. He knew I'd only ever help him.

Once he was standing on all fours, I ran my hands over his leg. No lumps or bumps or injuries. I straightened. "Tumpoo, what am I going to do with you?" I asked, looking into his deep brown eyes. He rubbed me with his head, bleated, then picked up a strand of my hair in his mouth and tugged.

"You monster," I said and jerked my hair from his mouth. "You got us in so much trouble. And you wrecked Mom's painting. She'll never forgive you for that." I put my arms around his neck. "You have to start behaving. I don't want to lock you in your stall all the time."

Tumpoo pulled away from me and headed toward the open door. Enough mushy stuff for him, I guess. I followed him until I reached Rusty, then stood beside my gray gelding and watched the moose pest join Twilight in the unfenced part of the meadow. As usual, he spread his front legs and stretched his short neck, and reeeaaached until he could just nibble the tips of the grass.

What was I going to do with him? Right now, he was neither horse nor moose. Would he ever fit in anywhere? Was I irreversibly damaging him by allowing him to hang out with the horses? But how could I stop him?

And worse, I could be causing the same damage, or more, by spending time with him myself.

I sighed and undid the cinch of Rusty's saddle, then pulled it from his sturdy back. Next I removed his bridle and carried the two into the tack room. I came out with brushes and a small bucket of oats, and found Rusty already grazing outside the barn door. He accepted the oats politely.

"I don't know what to do," I said aloud as I started to groom him. I didn't expect him to answer, even telepathically, as he doesn't understand English, but I felt better talking it through. "Mom likes having the door open in the summer, but we need some way to keep Tumpoo out of the house. Or even better, inside the pasture." The problem was it would take huge amounts of money to make the fence moose proof. Posts bought and transported and pounded. Roll after expensive roll of livestock wire strung. And then Tumpoo would probably just find some other way to escape – even good fences are pretty ineffective when faced with a wild moose who doesn't want to be stopped. So fixing the fence wasn't really a solution, even if we could afford it, which we couldn't.

But how else could we protect the house? The woodpile? The water trough?

The water trough was the easiest one. I always filled the water buckets in the stalls if the horses were locked in at night. I could just use those buckets all the time, leaving the big water trough dry. With the stall doors open to the pasture during the day, the horses would have access to their private water, plus Tumpoo would be encouraged to go to the lake for his, which was something he needed to learn anyway if he was ever going to become a wild moose.

Rusty bobbed his head to chase a fly away from his chest, and I moved behind him to comb his glossy dark tail.

Now what about the woodpile? What we really needed was a woodshed with a strong door. Since we didn't have that, maybe I could cut off his climbing access to the pile somehow… yes, that was the answer. If the woodpile was too tall for him to jump on to begin with, he wouldn't be able to knock it down – and I could make it taller by putting upright boards at both ends and restacking the wood yet again. Basically, I needed to turn the woodpile into a tall wall, right next to the windowless, doorless outside wall of our house.

Rusty snorted and took a couple of steps toward a new patch of grass and I followed him with the body brush in hand. He was looking so good, glimmering like shiny steel in the afternoon light.

I searched the unfenced part of the pasture. Where were my two miscreants? For a moment I didn't see them, but then I noticed Twilight's gold beneath the shade of the trees at the edge of the meadow, and beside her, a brown lump. They were both reclining, taking their afternoon nap. It was safe to keep thinking.

So what about the house?

What we needed was a way to open up the house

without allowing access for an errant moose. We could just open our windows, but both Mom and I liked more air than that when the weather was nice.

So I could either be sure to always lock Tumpoo up on the nicest days – which would really be too bad for him – or … we could open up *part* of our front door. Brilliant! We could cut the door in half horizontally, put on some extra hinges, and turn it into a Dutch door. Surely he wouldn't try to climb over the bottom half of the door if it was closed. We could make it as tall as the door in his stall, just to be sure. With Dutch doors, the worst that Tumpoo could do would be to stand with his head in the house and bawl for treats – and Mom with her broom would certainly stop that from happening too much.

I finished with the soft brush, then led Rusty to the pasture gate. He walked inside and nickered to Cocoa. His old friend looked up from where she grazed, bits of green poking from her mouth. Rusty sniffed at the dumped trough – I'd have to haul some water for their stalls right away – then he and Cocoa, two old comfy friends, wandered off, side by side. Soon, they too would be napping in the shade.

I grabbed the stall buckets, made the trek down to the lake and back, and placed the full buckets in the two stalls. Then I looked for Tumpoo and Twilight – still sleeping. And now, since I had a reprieve from animal antics and duties for a while, I would talk to Mom about my ideas. Afterward, I could get started on the woodpile.

Mom was still staring off into space, looking lost, when I walked into the house.

"Mom, I have the solution."

She looked at me with tired eyes. I explained how we could fix the water and wood situation, then made my suggestion of Dutch doors, to which I added that I always thought they looked cool anyway. "And I was wondering," I added, thinking this was my opportunity to ask for something I'd *always* wanted. "You know how I'm forever asking to keep one of your paintings? Well, can I have that one?" I pointed to the damaged canvas. "I don't care if it has a hole at the bottom. I love it."

Mom winced when she looked at the painting again. Then she climbed out of the chair, picked it up and held it in front of herself as she examined it. "I'd like you to have one that isn't ruined."

"It's *not* ruined. It's beautiful. And I could stitch up the canvas."

"But it'll always show."

"I don't care."

She looked at me. "Are you sure, honey? I'd like you to have a perfect one."

I smiled at her. "It *is* a perfect one, Mom. It was painted by you and it's a picture of Rusty and Twilight. How much better can it get?"

She seemed to melt, either because of my words or my smile. I guess I hadn't smiled at her much lately. "Then it's yours." Her voice was hushed.

A thrill shivered through my heart. Finally, I would have one of my mom's gorgeous, remarkable paintings to hang on my own wall. This one was extra special to me too because both Rusty and Twilight were in it, plus the painting was so fitting. Rusty and Twilight were my glorious pathway to a magical world of wild adventures and talking horses. And since I'd never have gotten the painting if it wasn't for Tumpoo, this one thing I was grateful to him for. The hole in the bottom corner was no big deal. In fact, it made the painting better in a way. It was Tumpoo's contribution, and the story of how the hole came to be only made the painting more interesting.

Mom carried the painting gingerly into my room as if it were the most fragile thing she'd ever held, even though the poor thing had just been through a war zone with Tumpoo rampaging through the house. I fetched a hammer and nail and minutes later, the painting was hanging on my wall, looking as stunning as I knew it would. The sad look on Mom's face lightened a bit as we stood back to look at it.

"It belongs here," she said, her voice soft. "This is its home." Then she looked around the rest of my room. Uh-oh.

"I'll clean my room right after the rest of the house is done," I said, quickly.

Mom turned back to the painting. "Enchanted. That's what I called it."

"It's perfect," I said, and breathed deep. My painting, Enchanted. "Thanks so much, Mom."

She put her arm around me and pulled me close,

and for a moment I leaned against her shoulder and closed my eyes. She smelled so good, like oil paints and lavender soap, just as she always did. Just for a moment, I felt the way I used to when I was a little kid and climbed on her lap and listened to her tell me about colors and brushes and lighting and how she believed that creating a painting was like casting spells.

A minute later we were picking up paint tubes and brushes, and when we finished in Mom's working area, she went into her bedroom to strip the bed while I went to check whether or not Tumpoo was still hanging out in the meadow with Twilight. He was, which kind of surprised me. Twilight must be feeling extra patient today if she hadn't run him off yet.

I moved reluctantly to the kitchen and grabbed the broom. It was disheartening to brush up all that flour and sugar and oatmeal. It all cost money and I knew that Mom stressed about money all the time these days. Even the loss of a bag of flour was bad.

I wiped off all the cans and knelt down to replace them on the shelves, then removed the ripped and dirty curtains from the front of the cupboards. Finally, I hauled water from the lake, heated it, and started to scrub. And as I wiped the cupboards and scrubbed the floors, something weird happened. I started to feel all sappy. Our house was just so little and cute and rustic, and, well, it was our *home* – and I was gloriously proud of it. I scrubbed harder. Polished more thoroughly. I started to hum.

"Evy?"

I stood up. Mom was in the doorway to her room.
Her face was white and her mouth a thin line. She was
wringing her hands, something she only did when she
was super stressed about something. Maybe she'd found
a pile of moose turds behind the door and wanted me to
clean it up.

"Yeah?"

She stared at me for a long moment, looking as if
she was trying to will words from between her clenched
teeth. When it didn't happen, she finally forced her
hands to her side. Then she spoke. "You can go."

"Go? Where?"

"To the..." Cough.

"What?"

"To the... to the rodeo."

"What? Really?" For a second I couldn't take it in.
"Oh, wow! Awesome!"

"But you promise me you won't wander away from
Kestrel or someone in her family, okay?"

"I promise."

"And you have to be back home by sunset, okay?"

"No problem."

"And I don't have much money to give you."

"All I need is enough to get into the rodeo, that's all."

Mom nodded, then turned back to her bedroom.

"Mom?"

She stopped. Turned back.

"Why are you letting me go?"

She tipped her head back and blinked for a moment, not wanting to cry again. I waited. When she spoke, her words were soft. "Because you're growing up. You're incredibly capable and resourceful, and I can trust you."

Wow. I didn't expect all that. And that's when the idea jumped into my head – now was the time to ask that *other* question. "Kestrel might be going away this fall to a boarding school in Vancouver. I… well… if I think it's the *right* thing to do, can I go too?"

A good way to phrase the question, I thought – until her pale face became impossibly whiter. She inhaled sharply and leaned on the doorpost, choked out an indistinguishable sound that I assumed meant, "No way, not ever, not in a million, trillion years," and then rushed into her room. You'd think I'd just told her I'd gotten a full body tattoo or was running away to Tibet to join a commune or something equally devastating. What was so terrible about boarding school in Vancouver? Other than my mom being a hermit. Other than her being afraid either of people in general or a specific *someone* or *something*, and thus hiding in the bush.

Oh, wait. There *was* that one other bad thing about Vancouver.

My dad had died there.

I could have kicked myself. I should've first told her the *what,* and then when that was okay – if it ever was okay – told her the *where*. Apparently, my dad was in a car accident in Vancouver, just months after I was born. My mom hardly ever spoke of him, and because she was reluctant to tell me about him, because I'd never known him, and because as far back as I could remember it had only been me and Mom, I didn't think about him much.

I did miss not having a dad in some ways, though. What kid wouldn't? It was especially hard when Kestrel joked with her dad, Seth. And sometimes I wondered what my dad was like. Was I like him in any way? Could he talk to horses too?

Feeling both terrible for upsetting my reclusive mother and irritated with her for being so easily upset, I left the house with the wash bucket in my hand. I threw the soapy water out onto the grass and then looked across the meadow. Twilight and Tumpoo were gone.

Twilight? Where are you?

Lake.

Tumpoo?

Watching him.

I felt my shoulders relax just a bit. My filly was keeping an eye on the calf for me. Fantastic. Had she realized that Tumpoo was causing too much trouble? If so, I was grateful. Maybe between me, Rusty, Twilight, and the new setup around the house, we'd keep him under control.

I walked down the porch steps and around the side of the cabin, the bucket in my hand. I really didn't need clean water to finish the floors, but I had to get outside for a bit. Some fresh air to help me think.

The whole time that I walked, watched Twilight and

Tumpoo splashing in the shallows, hauled more water, heated it again, and finished the floor, I thought – and not happy thoughts. I wanted to focus on the rodeo and being allowed to go, but I couldn't. Avoiding being separated from Kestrel for almost a year was far more important than one fun day at a rodeo. There might be a solution I was overlooking. Like maybe Mom would let me go *if* the school was somewhere other than Vancouver?

And where would we find the money? It would cost a lot.

But even if Mom didn't mind a boarding school in some other city and we could find the money, how would I convince Kestrel's parents to send her somewhere else? How would we find another school in time? It seemed an impossible task, and I wondered if I'd be smart to give up – but I'm not the type to surrender. Getting permission to go to the rodeo had made me optimistic. That had seemed unattainable too, but look what happened! Maybe this boarding school thing would work out too.

Rodeo time! At last!

Rusty shone like a new quarter, bright in the morning sun, as I saddled him. I'd brushed him for an hour yesterday evening and said goodnight with strict instructions not to get dirty. Talking to your horse can have great benefits – well, if the horse listens better than Twilight, anyway. She looked like a dirt ball, as if she'd rolled in the muddiest places on purpose. And maybe she had. I'd told her last night that she wasn't coming to the rodeo with us, and she'd been enormously peeved about it. The knowledge that Tumpoo was staying home too made no difference to her mood. Neither did the facts that she didn't like being around a lot of people and she'd have to spend a lot of the day tied up if she went. If Rusty and I were going, she wanted to go too, plain and simple.

With intermittent yawns, Mom saddled Cocoa. She was riding with me as far as Kestrel's ranch to make sure that Kestrel's parents, Seth and Elaine, knew I had to be home that night before sunset. When I rushed back inside the barn to say my goodbyes to Tumpoo and Twilight, Tumpoo bawled because he wanted *out now* and Twilight turned her bum toward me.

Riding away from the cabin and barn, I tried once more. *I am sorry, Twilight, but you would not like it. Honestly.*

Do not talk to me.

Yikes, she was really mad. I'd have to find some way to make it up to her later. Right now, all I wanted to think about was having the best day of my life – or best day so far!

The ride to Kestrel's went quickly with no Twilight or Tumpoo to wait for, go find, rescue, or check on. The only unusual thing that I sensed was the mustang stallion, but the far reaches of my hearing told me that he was grazing calmly in a meadow and seemed satisfied enough to stay there.

When we were a quarter mile from Kestrel's house, Mom reined Cocoa to a walk. Rusty slowed to match her pace, and when Mom stopped Cocoa, Rusty stopped too.

"Just a second," Mom said, then fell silent.

I waited, impatient for her to speak. She seemed to be having trouble forming the words. More serious talk. Great.

My bad feeling grew as seconds ticked past and she remained quiet. The only thing I could think and hope and pray was that she hadn't changed her mind about the rodeo.

"About what we were talking about the other day."
Another pause. "The boarding school. In Vancouver."
She almost choked when she said the word Vancouver.

Incredible! My miracle was going to happen. Mom
was going to give me permission to go!

"You wouldn't really like it," Mom said.

I blinked. That didn't sound like permission.

"I know you. You'd hate it. All the rules and
schedules and being monitored all the time. Controlled
every second."

This sounded suspiciously like what I'd told Twilight
last night. And I reacted just as Twilight did. "Maybe I'd
love it more than anything." I know that sounds obstinate,
but really, how could she know I'd hate it? Had she ever
been to boarding school? Well, maybe she had – I didn't
know – but even so, even if she was right and I wouldn't
like it, shouldn't I make that decision for myself?

"You love it here. Or I thought you loved it here,
anyway, with or without Kestrel."

"I *do* love it here, Mom," I said, my voice more
exasperated than I intended, "but that doesn't mean I
wouldn't like a chance to be a normal person once in
a while."

"Is it really *that* terrible, having an unusual life?"

Okay, so there was no answer for that... or maybe
there was. "I don't know. Since I'm *not* normal, since
I haven't *ever* had a normal life, how can I know if I'd
like to *be* normal?" I threw my hands up to accentuate
my point and Rusty snorted. "I don't even know what

normal is," I said with vehemence, then cut to the master stroke. "And I'm probably going to be weird my whole life because of growing up isolated from everyone except Kestrel, who now is leaving for her normal life, by the way. So what chance do I have of *ever* fitting in? No chance. I'm a weirdo, a total misfit – because of *you*."

Mom looked like I'd slapped her, which made me feel like crawling under a rock. But I couldn't back down. Not now. Not when she was so adamant about controlling every aspect of my life.

"We better get going," I said, trying hard to make my voice a bit softer. Maybe she'd know I felt sorry for being so mean without my actually saying it.

Mom just nodded and turned Cocoa. Five minutes later, we were riding into Kestrel's yard.

Twitchy was tied to the hitching post by the barn, saddled and looking like she'd resigned herself to stand there forever as Kestrel tried to force her mane to lie to the left side of her neck. Mom rode toward where Seth stood beside the truck, looking at his watch, and I turned off to help Kestrel. I already knew that her parents and two sisters were going in the truck. Kestrel and I wanted to ride our horses to the rodeo instead. We thought it would be more fun to have Rusty and Twitchy there, plus we had an ulterior motive.

"Hey," said Kestrel and smiled up at me, then looked at Twitchy's mane and grimaced. A line appeared on her forehead. "Mom says it's impossible. No one has ever been able to tame Twitchy's mane."

"She looks cute that way anyway," I said, and she did. The bay mare had a rumpled, huggable look to her, like a comfy grandma horse.

Kestrel stood back and eyed her handiwork, then shook her head. "I give up." She slipped the bridle onto the mare's head. Moments later, she was in the saddle, scowling down at Twitchy's mane. "It looks even worse now." She poked at the hair standing up like a rooster's tail.

"Just push it back to the right side," I suggested.

Kestrel leaned forward to shove the errant black mane to the right – and it stuck out straight to the side. I couldn't help but laugh, and moments later Kestrel was laughing too.

"We can stop by a creek on the way and wet it down," I said.

"Yeah. Let's go."

I yelled goodbye to Mom and waved, knowing she'd motion me to come over and then proceed to give me every instruction and caution she'd already told and retold to me over the last few days. When she just waved back – and a tiny wave at that – I felt horrible. She wasn't even going to lecture me again? Didn't she care?

I was about to go over anyway, thinking she'd feel better if she had the opportunity to tell it all to me again, when Elaine and Kestrel's older sisters, Mya and Nova, came out of the house.

"Hello, Laticia," Elaine said. "Are you sure you won't change your mind about coming?"

Mom turned her attention to Elaine, and knowing our opportunity to talk was over, I reined Rusty toward the big ranch gates. Then Kestrel and I were high-tailing it out of there.

We slowed to a ground eating lope when we were out of sight of the house. In less than two hours, we'd be at the rodeo. Butterflies battered the inside of my ribcage, making me feel totally sick with excitement.

Within ten minutes, Kestrel's family drove past us. I was extra glad we'd taken the horses as they honked and waved and disappeared around the corner in front of us. I needed time to prepare myself for all the noise and excitement of the day. I'd only ever been to town twice in my whole life – no, I'm not lying. Once was with Kestrel and her family, and the other time was with my Mom and Kestrel. Both times I went to the General Store, and once even bought a candy bar – oh wonder of wonders!

But never, ever had I been to a rodeo, or any other event, for that matter. I'd never seen or heard a crowd, though I'd certainly imagined them. The noise was going to be fantastically cool and energizing. There would be more than a couple of people talking at once. There'd even be cheering and yelling and whooping and clapping. Kestrel had told me about the rodeo announcer and how he'd probably be telling bad jokes and hamming things up with the rodeo clown. And there might even be music. That would be awesome. Except for my own off-key singing, which doesn't really count, and Kestrel's CD player, I'd never even *heard* music. Unbelievable and beyond bizarre, I know.

And not only would there be a ton of cool human things going on today, there'd be lots of horse happenings, too. Just thinking about it all made me want to hurry. I asked Rusty to go a bit faster and he drew abreast of Twitchy. Kestrel grinned over at me and then both horses moved into a gallop. Twitchy even had her ears forward. We all wanted to get there. I felt like I'd been waiting my entire life to do this one thing. This was my launch into the real world. And it could only lead to being allowed to do *more* things, go to *more* events, have *more* social adventures. Oh, yeah!

The town was hopping with activity. People, horses, and dogs were everywhere. Kestrel seemed to know everyone as we rode through the streets toward the rodeo grounds. I echoed her "hi" to everyone and grinned until my cheeks ached. Everyone looked at me like they were trying to figure out who I was, but I didn't care. I could hear the beat of distant music – *yes!* – and as we came closer, yelling and cheering. The sun beat down, hot and sultry. Not a cloud in the sky. Life, in this moment, was perfect. Or almost. Horse emotions slipped into my mind like water, filling it up, drowning my ability to listen to people. I wanted to listen to the horses too and especially didn't want to close Rusty out, but as we got closer the voices and emotions became louder and more insistent. Then, as I guessed would happen, I felt my first wave of dizziness.

Feelings are much more powerful and consuming than mere human speech.

Regretfully, I used my old trick – I closed the door on my horse sense, or almost. I left it open a crack so I could hear Rusty's voice. I'd still be able to sense the strongest emotions too, though they would be muted. And I'd be able to sense any other horses with the ability to think in abstract thought, like Rusty. There wouldn't be many, if any. Most horses are purely and beautifully emotional creatures.

I reached out to touch all that I could hear with my diminished sense, so I knew what I'd be dealing with – and there were only three more abstract thinkers in the hundred or so horses at the rodeo. One was with the broncos and another was a young colt, a yearling. The third was barely there; its conscious thoughts were fuzzy as though muddied or far away. Or groggy maybe. You know that feeling when you sleep too long? I'd never felt that from a horse before, and it seemed strange. But with only those three and Rusty to hear, I'd be able to concentrate on what the humans around me were doing and saying, no problem. Awesome!

When we reached the rodeo grounds, we rode straight to the competitor's entrance. This was the one secret I'd kept from my mom. We'd brought our horses for another reason. Yeah, it would be more fun to have them here, but we'd also entered them in the horse games that were to be held after the main rodeo events were over. At three o'clock, the fun for the kids would begin. There was the Barrel Race, even though they had a separate race for the professional Barrel Racers with the rodeo, plus four other events: Pole Bending, Stakes, Scurry, and the Egg and Spoon Race.

I hadn't known about the games until last week when Kestrel came to visit, so I'd only had time to practice one event, the Barrel Race. It had the most prize money – one hundred dollars, donated by a local business – so that was the one we practiced. I still wanted to enter Rusty in all the other games too though, just for fun.

Kestrel and Twitchy were pros at the games. Last year they'd won both the Pole Bending and the Stakes. Twitchy had competed with both of Kestrel's sisters when they were younger, and from what I'd heard, she'd been good too.

Inside the competitors' compound, we greeted about a billion strangers – or they were strangers to me, anyway – and then found a shady spot for the horses. They were still a bit hot from the gallop in, so we unsaddled them and then went to find Kestrel's truck. In the back, we measured oats into buckets, and after Rusty and Twitchy were contentedly munching away and we'd hauled some water for them, we walked over to the arena to watch the rodeo.

"Hey, Evy! Kestrel!"

I spun around. No one knew me here, so who could be calling my name? Kestrel's elbow found my ribs as we both spied Jon walking toward us. I urgently hoped and wished and desired that – please, please – my face wasn't as red as it felt.

"Hi, Jon," said Kestrel, in her teasing voice.

"Hi," I said, wishing I could think of something witty and brilliant to say.

"When did you get here?"

Okay, so he wasn't saying anything exceptionally bright either. Maybe I was okay. "Just barely," I said and pointed. "Our horses are over there."

Jon looked over at Rusty and Twitchy. "Oh no, you brought Twitchy," he said.

"You bet. And I'm going to totally beat you this year. Again." Thankfully, Kestrel was gloating now, something she preferred to teasing.

"I don't know. She's getting old," said Jon. "And I've been working with Coal." Coal was Jon's black gelding. I'd met him a few months ago and he seemed like a kind, surefooted horse, but not overly racy. Not that Twitchy was any speed demon.

"I'm entering this year too," I volunteered.

"Oh great," Jon said, dismayed. "Maybe I should…" His voice trailed off as he looked at us, obviously wondering if he should tell us something. I couldn't help but think how cute he looked when he felt confused. "Come with me," he finally said. "I want to show you something."

We followed Jon as he weaved his way through the other competitors and their trailers and horses.

Hello, human girl.

I almost jumped out of my skin. I turned to see a paint yearling tied to a trailer. He was looking at me.

Hello, human girl, he repeated.

Hello, I replied hesitantly. Other than Rusty and Twilight, I'd never had another horse speak to me. And I hadn't even spoken to this one first. How did he know I could hear him?

Water.

I walked over to him and looked down at his bucket. It was empty. *Sure,* I said.

Over there. An image popped into my head of a water pump near the trees where Rusty and Twilight lounged.

I know, I said, a little peeved that he thought I was stupid. *Be right back.* I picked up his bucket and fetched his water, thinking about how bizarre it was. This little yearling must be a protégé of language, a horse genius. And he thought I was his slave because I could hear his commands.

His owner was brushing him when I got back with the water. The man looked at me, perplexed, when I put the water in front of the colt – who wasted no time plunging his nose into the cool liquid.

"Sorry," I said to the man. "He just looked thirsty." I heard a sniggering snort from the colt. He thought this was funny. "He's a beautiful colt," I added, backing up.

"Uh, thanks," the guy said, still staring at me like I was an alien or something.

"Evy, *there* you are. Come on!" Kestrel grabbed my arm and pulled me away. We passed people doing things and looking busy, and horses relaxing and not speaking to me – thank goodness – and then came to the other side of the competitors' area.

Jon was running his hands down the slender legs of a tall chestnut mare. A grumpy man looked on as Kestrel and I stood silently, waiting. Finally, Jon straightened.

"Give me a minute," he said to the man and the three of us walked away. Out of earshot, we stopped and huddled.

"So what do you think?"

"About the horse?" I asked, like a genius.

"Of course, about the horse."

"She looks fine to me."

"Me too," added Kestrel. "But isn't that a Three Bar Hoop brand on her? I heard that their horses are crazy."

"Just high strung and sensitive," Jon said defensively, then he sighed. "But I know what you're saying. She's cheap, so there might be something wrong with her. Maybe she's *really* high strung and sensitive."

"In other words, crazy," said Kestrel.

"If that's the case," I interjected, glad that I finally had something smart to say. "It's good to try her in a stressful place, like here, before you decide."

Jon nodded. "You're right."

Slowly, we walked back to the man. Jon stopped in front of him. "I'll take her if you let me try her out today. If I like her, I'll give you the full amount."

The man grinned. "It's a deal." He held out his hand and Jon shook it.

"I'll be back in a minute," Jon said to the guy, who didn't look so grumpy now.

"I need to tie Coal somewhere cool, since he's just

going to be waiting around today," Jon explained as soon as we left the mare.

"Why don't you put him with our horses?" I offered, refusing to look at Kestrel as I said this. No doubt she'd think I was flirting.

"Good idea," said Jon, a little too quickly. "It's nice and shady over there and he'll like the company."

We reached the black gelding and I stroked his neck as Jon untied him. He really was a nice horse. In some ways, he was like a younger version of Rusty; kind, smart, and very steady.

Kestrel and I walked on one side of Coal and Jon on the other, as we led him to where our horses waited. Halfway there, Kestrel leaned over and whispered in my ear, "You two are so cute together."

I thought about slugging her, but that would've been too obvious. Instead, I decided to be a grown up, and, you know, act mature. I looked around Coal's head at Jon. "How come you want another horse?" I asked. "You're not going to sell Coal, are you?"

"Never. I need another cow horse. I got a job working cattle over the summer and Coal gets pretty tired when I take him out every day." We reached the fence and he tied the gelding's lead rope so he had plenty of slack. "The ranch where I work doesn't have any horses to spare."

"I wish we had a good horse for sale," said Kestrel, "but we only have three. Twitchy, and Mom and Dad's horses."

"And we only have Rusty and Mom's horse, and Twilight, who'd be supremely ticked off if I even thought of selling her." Jon looked at me strangely, and I clamped my mouth shut. What a weird thing to say. Mom really did need to let me out in public more often so I could get some practice talking to people.

"Twilight's a little independent," Kestrel explained, taking pity on me. "Hey, we should go watch some events. You coming, Jon?"

"In a while. I want to spend some time with the mare first. I might bring her over here to meet Coal too."

"Okay. Catch you later."

Kestrel grabbed my arm and pulled me toward the rodeo arena.

"I'm so stupid," I moaned, once out of Jon's earshot. "Everything I say is dumb."

"No way. You did fine. Besides, you don't like him, so what do you care?" Kestrel laughed, knowing she had me.

I nodded, hoping that what Kestrel said was actually true and that Jon didn't think I was too weird. A little oddness might be okay, but not *too* much.

The saddle bronc event was in full swing when we arrived. We found seats on the bleachers and joined the yelling, cheering mass of humanity watching the horses and cowboys battle it out in the arena. Some cowboys were thrown, but most rode the eight seconds they were supposed to. The horses sure could buck! It made me nervous about the first time I'd ride Twilight. I'd have to get her to promise me she wouldn't buck before I got on her. There was no way I could ride like these guys.

I felt a sudden and intense increase of butterflies hammering against my stomach walls – and then the gate swung open and a big bay pounded the dirt.

Head down, tuck, and heels snap up. Spin around. Pitch right. Pitch right again. Man thinks right again, so straight up, kick, hang left! Wham!

The unlucky cowboy soared through the air like he'd been shot from a catapult. He landed in a poof of dust as the bay started his victory buck across the arena, the two pick-up men right behind him. As the cowboy regained his feet, he moved as if every muscle, bone, and sinew in his body ached.

The bay finished his victory pass, then, suddenly bored of the whole procedure, allowed the men on horses to believe they were herding him toward the exit gate. As he passed the cowboy he'd thrown, who was still leaving the arena, I could feel his smugness. He'd totally won. Ha! I almost laughed out loud when I felt his merriment, but thankfully, remembered just in time that there were other people around who could actually hear me.

We watched the steer wrestling and the bareback broncs, and when the calf roping began, went to grab a late lunch. My first burrito! Jon joined us on the grass near the concession booth and told us that all the horses were resting, including the mare – though of course I already knew that from Rusty.

Jon was pretty happy that his potential new horse seemed so calm. As we talked and laughed and I ate my burrito, I felt the smart colt who had earlier demanded water looking for me. He was bored and wanted me to come entertain him. Great. I hoped that he didn't realize he could call me from a distance, or I'd never hear the end of him. I wanted to relax and have fun, not be a slave to another demanding youngster – I got my fill of that at home with Twilight.

"Bull riding is next, folks," the announcer said, and then continued to give details which I didn't bother listening to.

"Come on, Evy. You *have* to see this. It's, well, it's bull riding," said Kestrel, jumping up.

"You're so eloquent," I teased, but I was right behind her as we three and the others who'd been eating rushed toward the bleachers.

The bull riding was everything I'd expected it to be, but more terrifying. One cowboy got his hand stuck in the straps, and after the bull threw him he flopped around on the bull's side like a rag doll. The bull wouldn't allow the pick-up men and horses near him, so they couldn't help the poor guy. It wasn't until the clown ran in front of the bull, flashing a big striped umbrella, that the bull was distracted enough for one of the pick-up men to run his horse alongside, reach down and jerk on the strap, and thus free the bull rider.

Another cowboy was almost trampled after being thrown. The only thing that saved him was that he hit the dirt near the fence and scrambled up the rails a millisecond before the snorting, stomping dragon reached him. One bull tried to gore his fallen cowboy. He rolled the man along with his horns a bit, then was distracted by the clown – and the cowboy jumped up and ran to the fence as if the devil was right behind him. The crowd loved it, every second. And except for a heart-seizing moment or two or three, I did too. Even the bulls looked like they were having a great time; I guess it was the perfect way to get out their aggressions. The only creatures that didn't seem happy were the cowboys who lost, but they knew what they were getting into when they signed up. So as long as they weren't hurt, I couldn't feel too sorry for them.

And then the last bull unseated his cowboy, chased him, caught him and gave him a toss, and then decided to go snort at the crowd. He ran along the other side of the fence, all red and vicious and watching us with his little black eyes – I'm sure he wished he could gore us all – and then the pick-up men ran him out of the arena and the rodeo was over.

Game time!

Jon, Kestrel, and I hurried back to the horses, and laughed and talked as we brushed them. The horses became excited as they caught our eagerness – except for Jon's potential new horse, that is. Her eyes were half closed and her ears flopped sideways. She seemed like she'd be a good horse to ride during an earthquake. She did stamp a hoof now and then, though, and when Jon tightened the cinch on her saddle, she raised her head a fraction. If the man was selling her to get rid of her, maybe her flaw was being *too* relaxed. Or, in another word, lazy.

Jon mounted in one smooth movement. The horse stood like a rock. He signaled her lightly to go and she sighed. He asked her again, firmly, and she turned obediently toward the arena.

"She seems level headed," Kestrel said as we followed them.

Jon looked back. "Maybe a bit too relaxed."

"How old is she supposed to be?" I asked.

"Only six. She should liven up in a few minutes. She was tied there quite a while."

I didn't mention that Rusty and Twitchy had been tied just as long, yet seemed to have plenty of energy. Instead, I held Rusty back as we followed Jon and his horse through the arena gate. The horse games weren't set up yet, and other kids were using the arena to warm up their mounts.

Rusty and I did a couple of walk-trot-lope circuits of the arena and then we exited the arena. Kestrel and Twitchy stood just outside the gate, so we joined them, and together we watched Jon and his mare. He stopped her, backed her, walked and trotted her in circles both ways, and finally broke into a lope. The mare moved sluggishly but perfectly. She didn't miss a beat when Jon asked her to make a flying lead change. She did a slow motion sliding stop, then surged into an obedient, if unenergetic lope. A couple minutes later, Jon rode back to us, smiling.

"You're looking nervous, Kestrel," he said, laughing. "You know I'm going to beat you today in the Barrel Race."

"Don't be so sure. Twitchy's got lots of speed left in her still."

"Yeah, when she's heading toward her oats."

"Well, your new horse isn't any speed demon. She looks like she's asleep again."

And she did, except for one ear that now kept up

85

a regular flicking. But Jon was unphased. "She'll run Twitchy into the ground. Wait and see."

As I listened to this exchange, I couldn't help but notice they were both overlooking Rusty. What was he? Pickled herring? Apparently not a threat, in their minds, anyway. Well, we'd see who's the best – of *all* of us.

"All those interested in watching our talented young folks, please return to the arena," drawled the announcer over the loudspeaker. He didn't sound nearly as thrilled to be announcing the kid's games as he did for the rodeo. "Their events are about to begin."

The very first event was the Pole Bending race. You race to the last of six poles, all set in a straight line, turn around the sixth pole and then weave your horse back through them all. You turn again at the first pole and weave back through all six, and then turn around the sixth pole once more and race straight for the finish line. The fastest wins, and if you tip over a pole you get a five second penalty.

Rusty and I were the second to run. We did okay, but then Twitchy totally blew us out of the competition. She didn't run too fast, but wow, could she move around those poles! Jon said something confident to us before riding the chestnut mare into the arena, but returned from his run looking sheepish. The horse did okay, but she'd fought him when he asked her to turn at the sixth pole. At least she'd run fast on the way to the finish line – surprisingly fast, actually – but then she didn't want to stop. If there hadn't been a fence there, I wondered if she would've kept going.

"Good thing you're trying her out now," I said to Jon when he reined the mare to stand beside us. "She might be a runaway."

He leaned down and patted the mare on her hot shoulder. "She did okay." The mare snorted. "And besides, she's a cow horse. The guy said she's never done anything like this before."

"She probably isn't used to the crowds and noise either," I added, because Jon was right. The mare had done okay – okay enough to have beaten Rusty. He'd done the turns without fighting, but the mare's sprint to the finish line had given her the faster time.

Kestrel and Twitchy won the Pole Bending and then Jon and the chestnut came second in the Stakes – which was a miracle, by the way. They walloped the end pole, hard, on their last turn. I'm not sure what made it stay up, but stay up it did, so no penalty. Add to that the mare's now obvious love of running and they squeaked out a time just one tenth of a second faster than Twitchy and Kestrel.

Rusty and I weren't much competition to the leaders, but we didn't do too badly in the Scurry event, which was jumping your horse over three eighteen-inch jumps, turning around a pole, and then jumping back over the jumps. Kestrel did well too, but Jon and his new horse were terrible. The chestnut couldn't jump to save her life – not that she actually tried. She looked like she was getting exasperated with all this gaming as she ran through the three jumps. Jon struggled to make her turn around the pole and then she raced back over the fallen jumps, going about a hundred miles an hour. When Jon asked her to slow down, she started shaking her head in protest.

No!

Was she the third horse that I'd heard? The groggy one?

Do not want to!

She was! And her confusion was falling away. Her mind was growing clearer – and in it I could see a singular purpose: to get away. Not just from the events, not just from all the shouting and excitement of the rodeo, but away from *everything*. Away from civilization. Away from anything human. More than anything, this formerly calm and unflappable mare wanted to escape her life.

Jon and the mare burst from the arena and swept toward Kestrel and me. The other horses and riders scattered in front of them like mice before a cat.

"Control your horse, please," the announcer droned, as if Jon wasn't already trying.

Finally, the mare reached us and stopped, wild-eyed, then pushed up next to Rusty. For some reason, she felt safer beside him. I didn't mind, at least until she squished Jon's and my knees together. Hard. "Ouch!"

Jon's face turned red. "Sorry. I don't know what's wrong with her." He pulled on the left rein, and the mare jumped over a foot, then did a little hop and stood still.

"She seems to like Rusty, anyway," I said over the announcer's voice. "Maybe he can help her calm down."

"I don't think she likes rodeos."

I was about to suggest that maybe it was more than that, when Kestrel said, "Evy, you came in third!"

A flush of pleasure ran through my body. "Oh wow, I don't believe it! What did you get, Kestrel?"

She looked a little embarrassed as she replied. "Second. Sorry."

"Hey, don't be. I'm happy with third. I didn't think I'd get anything." How cool! My first win and after only three races. Rusty and I would get a ribbon, and maybe even five bucks in prize money. I couldn't stop smiling.

"Egg and Spoon Racers, enter the arena," said the announcer.

"Let's go," Kestrel said to me, grinning back.

"Are you doing this one?" I asked Jon, hoping the answer was no. The mare had calmed a bit, thanks to Rusty's steady presence, but who knew how long it would last? Her agitation was still there; I could feel it like a hornet buzzing in my brain.

"I'm going to see if Jake has a partner yet," he said, looking back at a dark haired boy on a skinny bay. He'd done well in all the games so far. Unless Jon's horse messed things up for them by jumping the fence and disappearing over the horizon, they'd probably be our biggest competitors.

"Good luck."

"You too."

Rusty and I followed Kestrel into the arena and we positioned ourselves with one of us at each end. Jon and

Jake were the last two to line up. It was a competitive looking field. Nine teams.

The starting pistol fired. Cheering started in the stands. A shudder of alarm rushed through me and I realized it was coming from Jon's mare. I had to shut her out if I was going to concentrate on this race, though I hated to do it. I wouldn't be able to hear Rusty then, either.

Sorry, Rusty, I thought to him. *Must shut off listening.*

I understand.

You are awesome.

Yes.

I smiled and patted his neck, then shut my mind completely to the horses. Thank goodness I'd learned how to do that last winter. I'd be a total wreck now if not for what I had learned back then. No matter how harrowing that experience had been, it was totally worth it. Not to mention that I got Twilight out of it.

Kestrel and Twitchy, along with all the other half teams, were still walking toward us, their spoons held in front of them, their eggs wobbling in each shallow hollow. This race was perfect for Twitchy – steady and slow. If Rusty and I did as well, we'd win it.

Then Kestrel noticed that Jake's skinny bay was drawing ahead of her. She signaled to Twitchy and the old mare moved, slow and lethargic, into a rocking horse lope. The egg didn't even shudder on Kestrel's spoon. The girl to their left tried to copy Kestrel's slick move, but her horse lurched into a trot, bouncing the egg out of its cradle and splatting it on her saddle horn. Another team's egg hit the ground.

Then Jake asked his horse to go faster too. But instead of loping, the bay moved into a smooth trot, with long supple strides. Their egg was wiggling, but not falling. And the pair was gaining on Kestrel and Twitchy!

"Faster, faster," I shrieked, but my voice was lost in the crowd. Apparently, the spectators loved this race. I'd never heard such a racket. I guess raw eggs spraying hapless contestants brings out the noise in people – me included.

By the time the first riders drew near, there were only five teams left in the race and the eliminated players, covered in varying degrees of yolk, had already withdrawn to the sidelines. Jake had a thin lead over Kestrel and two riders were about ten yards behind them. Only one was way back – a little girl, who looked about four years old, riding the slowest, widest, cutest pony I'd ever seen. If the egg had fallen on him, I'm sure it would have been safely sheltered on his soft, cuddly self.

And then Jake reached Jon. I was still screaming at Kestrel to hurry, thinking they were going to quickly transfer the egg and then Jon's horse would hustle off, smoothly and miraculously, to victory. Unrealistic, yes, but not *completely* impossible.

Then Kestrel was there. I hardly breathed as I took the spoon handle.

Kestrel didn't immediately release her hold.

"Remember, slower is better," she advised, loudly, so I could hear her above the crowd. "It's better than not getting there at all."

I nodded.

"And look only at the egg." She released her hold and I asked Rusty to walk. Slower is better. Slower is better. Watch the egg. Only the egg. But what if Jon was passing me? I passed the two riders in third and fourth place coming toward me, and there was still no sign of Jon drawing alongside. In my peripheral vision, I could see only the crowd and the supremely cute pony with his equally endearing rider. Maybe Jon and Jake hadn't transferred their egg yet. Maybe no one had. Maybe we were going to win!

Visions of the twenty-five dollar prize danced through my head. What would I spend it on? Kestrel and I could go shopping today at the General Store before we headed home. Surely Mom wouldn't confiscate any candy I bought with hard earned winnings.

Yelling erupted behind me. Not the happy, cheering kind. The scared kind.

Watch the egg. Only the egg.

Kestrel screamed.

Automatically, I tried to sense Twitchy and…

Escape! Run from this madness. Can take no more!

Jon's mare's rage and terror was followed instantly by a hundred other horse emotions, Twitchy's fear included. I almost tumbled from Rusty's back with the force of the thoughts and sensation. To stop my eyes from rolling back in my head, I squeezed my eyelids shut, then struggled to stop the flood ripping through my mind. Bit by bit, I fought it back. Bit by bit, I stemmed the deluge. Bit by bit, I became myself again.

I opened my eyes to find myself clutching Rusty's mane. I tasted blood, so bent over the ground and spit. It was red. I must have bitten my lip.

Rusty nickered with concern and I patted him shakily on his shoulder. He was probably asking me questions, but I couldn't open up my horse-mind to hear him. Not with the mare right there, being overwhelmed. Still dazed, I raised my hand to wipe my mouth, to discover the spoon still clutched in my white-knuckled fist. No more blood when I wiped, thank goodness. However, the egg was now a spray of white and yolk and shattered eggshell on the ground. And on my knee. Great.

"Oh my God!" Caroline's shriek came from the stands. Caroline is Jon's mom. "Somebody do something!"

Finally in command of myself again, I spun Rusty around to see the third and fourth placed competitors, eggless and staring at Jon's horse as it continued to act completely and totally berserk: rearing, bucking, neighing, plunging, leaping. Twitchy and Kestrel were halfway across the arena, so I guessed the mare had run or kicked or stampeded near them, scaring them.

Rusty leapt forward into a gallop the second I asked him, but Jake acted before I could get there. He pushed his tough little bay up next to the freaking mare. Jon grabbed him around the waist, just like the bronc riders did when they wanted to dismount, and when Jake reined his horse away Jon was pulled from the mare's back. He hung at the bay's side for a moment, then landed lightly on the ground.

By the time I got there, it was over. But the mare didn't understand that she'd won. She was still going totally nuts. Bucking. Pitching. Striking. She leapt so hard to one side that her hooves flew from under her and she came thudding down onto her side. Moments later, she was up and high-tailing it past Kestrel to the far side of the arena. She crashed into the fence, but not through it, and fell again, then she scrambled to her hooves, slower this time, and stood stunned as we all stared at her in shock.

"Jon! Jon! Are you okay?" Caroline was running toward us.

"I'm fine, Mom," said Jon. "Really."

"You're *not* fine. I saw what happened. How can you say you're fine?"

Caroline wasn't fine, that's for sure. I looked sympathetically at Jon. He was totally embarrassed. First, publicly thrown, and then fussed over by his mother. Things couldn't get much worse for him. He didn't need me hanging around witnessing his shame.

Besides, the mare needed me. She might be injured. And I wanted to find out what had happened to make her freak out so badly. I opened the door to my horse senses just a crack.

Must escape. Don't belong. Flee from monsters. Flee!

Monsters? Now we humans were monsters? I had to help her.

"Evy?"

On one level, I heard Kestrel's bemused voice as we passed her, but I didn't have enough human sense to form words to answer her. Rusty continued to the far end of the arena where the mare stood, still too dazed to move. Yet.

Stay away! Stay away! This is only a meager interpretation of the revulsion she felt for me as I approached. Me, the horrendous human.

I stopped Rusty. I was going to have to talk to her. This may not seem like a big thing since I talk to horses every day, but it was. Huge, in fact. I only ever talked to Rusty and Twilight, with few exceptions – one being a wild mare that almost died after my brief greeting blasted through her brain, scaring her into hurting herself. But this mare was already frightened beyond reason. We had nothing to lose.

Name is Evy. Horse is Rusty. Your name? I asked, speaking as simply as possible.

Sheer terror lanced through her heart and I felt like my own was going to seize up. For a few seconds, all I could do was concentrate on breathing.

Do not be afraid, I eventually managed to add through the reflection of her terror. Then, *Why are you scared? Tell me. I will try to help.* Okay, so horses don't understand "try." *I will help,* I slowly amended, hoping she'd understand. Hoping that I *could* help her.

Help? A spark of hope, just a tiny, tiny spark, next to her raging bonfire of panic.

Yes. I will help.

Must escape. Help escape?

Where must you go?

Visions crowded my mind, visions of wandering wild lands, grazing untamed meadows, running at will, splashing through creeks, playing in snow, and most powerful than them all, having foals that would never be taken from her.

"Evy, what are you doing?" Kestrel said beside me.

"Just a sec."

"Are you crying?"

I raised my hand to my cheek. I was. I was crying the tears the mare couldn't cry herself. The man who was selling her had controlled every aspect of her life since she was four years old, when he brought her in from the range. She'd been strong during the cruel breaking in. She'd withstood the unkind voice, the meager rations, his roughness. But when he'd taken her foal from her side – as her baby screamed to her to save him – and she'd been unable to do anything to stop the man, the fire of desperation and hatred had flared inside her.

I will do my best to help you. But you must trust me. You must do as I ask first. Will you?

I dismounted Rusty and waited. Slowly, the horse turned her head and for the first time, really looked at me. Her eyes drank in the details of my body, her nose investigated my smell, her ears zeroed in on my breathing. She tried to sense the beating of my heart. Her mind probed mine and I tried opening myself a bit more to her – without letting in all the other horse voices – so she could know I was trustworthy.

And then she said, *yes*. A quiet singular agreement, but packed with power.

Thank you, I replied, and sighed. Thank goodness this was going to be resolved. I didn't want her to be hurt anymore. I didn't want her to hurt Jon. I only wanted everyone to be happy, and thank goodness, she recognized that.

"Be careful, Evy," Kestrel said behind me when I stepped toward the mare.

"She's okay now," I said. "See how relaxed she looks?" Even though she really didn't, I needed to say something. When I reached the mare's side, I stroked her cheek.

No touching.

Sorry.

I took her reins. She followed me – nervous and on edge, but still followed me – back to Rusty. Kestrel looked on in amazement as I mounted my horse.

"What did you do to her?"

"I just waited for her to calm down, that's all," I said to Kestrel, and smiled. "Really, most of it is Rusty. She trusts him."

"Well, he's a trustworthy guy."

As we rode back toward the gate, I felt overwhelmed by my promise to the mare. She believed she'd finally found someone who had the power to help her – and I still had no idea what to do. All I knew was that I had a lot less power and influence than she thought I did.

We made a detour around the group still arguing in the middle of the arena, and when we passed them, they didn't look over. I was infinitely glad. Jon was trying to convince his mom that the horse just didn't like games, that she'd still be an awesome cowhorse. Caroline was still yelling that there was no way he'd ever, ever, ever own that horse. Everyone else looked on with serious faces, injecting their opinions whenever they could. It was kind of bizarre, actually.

And then, beyond them, I noticed something hilarious. Slowly but surely, a second fat pony, looking just as squishy and soft and adorable as the first, was crossing the finish line. His tiny rider sat straight and proud on his back, one hand held high in victory and the spoon clutched firmly in her other. And glowing like a white beacon was the egg, nestled as snug in the spoon as if it were in a nest. The four-year-olds had won the race.

"And we have a winner!" said the announcer, interrupting the argument between Jon, Caroline, and all the opinionated onlookers.

I scanned the people in the stands as Kestrel and I escorted the mare toward the arena gate. Her owner wasn't there yet. Hopefully he wouldn't hear of the mishap for a while. I needed time to come up with a plan.

The announcer announced the winners of the Egg and Spoon Race, followed by, "All contestants for the Barrel Race, get ready!"

My heart lurched, and for a moment, I couldn't breathe.

"Evy! What on earth are you doing?" Jon's voice came from behind me.

I stopped Rusty. Jon was striding after us, looking flabbergasted.

"Is that... did you just... is that the crazy mare?"

I nodded.

"What did you *do* to her?" he asked, approaching Rusty on his far side.

"Nothing. Just waited for her to calm down."

Jon shook his head and looked sadly over Rusty's withers at the mare. "I can't buy her now. My mom freaked."

"I know. Sorry."

"Me too."

"You don't want her anyway," Kestrel said, in her chipper voice. She hates it when anyone feels bad, so always looks on the bright side of things. "I mean, she goes from half dead to a crazed beast in an hour? Not a good sign."

"You're probably right." Jon sighed. "Well, I'll catch you later." He hurried through the gates ahead of us, and Kestrel and I asked our horses to walk on.

"*Please* empty the arena," the announcer begged, sounding more than a little miffed.

"You know what? I think she might have been drugged," I said to Kestrel as I guided Rusty behind the bleachers. "That guy knew she was afraid and mad and I think that's why he wants to sell her. And so he doped her into calmness."

"That's sick." Kestrel sounded instantly outraged.

We led the mare to a quiet corner and I dismounted Rusty to tie her up.

Wait here. Return soon, I told her.

She didn't disagree or agree, so I assumed she was agreeing, and I wrapped her reins around the fence post. I took off the saddle and blanket and flopped them over the top rail and was about to give her a pat on the shoulder when I remembered her no touching rule. It seemed weird to walk away without patting her first, but I made myself do it. I mounted Rusty and Kestrel and I started back to the arena.

Wildfire.

I turned back. *What?* Then I remembered that I'd asked her name earlier. *Beautiful.*

"She looks so scared," Kestrel said, following my gaze, and it was true that the mare did look frightened. Only I knew she was way beyond frightened. The poor thing actually expected horrible monsters to attack at any second, because to her, monsters meant humans, and the worse monster of all was her owner. "And she's got a bad reputation now," Kestrel continued. "No one will buy her."

"I know," I said, and almost added, *except me.* I couldn't tell Kestrel yet, not until I knew if my fledgling plan would work or not. There was only one way to save the mare. Only one way to help her.

"I wonder if Jon went to get Coal?" Kestrel asked on our way back to the arena.

"I hope so," I said, even though he would just be more competition.

When we reached the arena fence, the other riders made room for us – and we all watched glumly as a girl with long brown hair rode a fleet footed pinto through the cloverleaf pattern of the Barrel Race. The pinto was so fast that the girl's hair and the horse's long black and white striped mane and tail blew straight out behind them. And that horse could turn too. The team shot over the finish line, and moments later, the announcer read out their time. No, their speed hadn't been an illusion. We were all toast.

Then the announcer called my name.

Next! We were up next! Oh. My. Gosh. An entire colony of butterflies swirled upward in my stomach and I suddenly needed to pee. It was going to have to wait, though. We were next!

Kestrel put her hand on my shoulder. "Good luck."

"Thanks. I need it."

Kestrel just nodded. I wished she'd lied. She could've said that I'd blow the competition away, no problem. She could've said that the pinto was a loser. Not that it would've made any difference to how good or bad I did – you can still only run as fast as you can run – but it would've made me feel better.

"Come on, Rusty. Let's go," I managed to choke through the butterflies winging up my throat. Rusty pranced into the arena, eager to run, and stopped at the starting place.

"Anytime you're ready," the announcer said.

I held the reins tight. I wasn't remotely ready.

Just hold on. Balance, said Rusty.

I was so nerved up, I barely heard him.

Hold on! Balance! Rusty repeated, forcefully.

I blinked. What did he mean? Not rein him? Not position him to correctly turn the barrels? Not tell him when to slow down or speed up? Was I just a passenger?

Okay. I could do that.

"Anytime now," the announcer repeated, sounding bored and irritated.

Okay, I am ready. I grabbed Rusty's mane.

My gelding leapt forward. Good thing he told me to hang on. We were at the first barrel before I finished inhaling and I swear my foot brushed the ground when he swept around it, he was leaning into the turn so hard. Then on to the next. I clung to his mane as he turned without an inch to spare between us and the barrels, then accelerated toward the last barrel in the cloverleaf pattern. It was the farthest away, but it seemed we were there in less than two heartbeats. Another ground scraper as we turned the barrel and then he was lunging for home, each stride the supreme effort. He'd never run so fast, not with me on his back. I didn't know he could go so fast, actually. He was beyond amazing.

We whipped past the finish line and slowed to a trot, both gasping like we'd just run a marathon. I slid from his back, weak as a caterpillar, and threw my arms around his neck.

Amazing! No – more! Stupendous! Fantastic! Incredible! Tears prickled my eyes. How did I ever get so lucky to have Rusty as a best horsey friend?

"Evy! That was amazing!" Kestrel's voice echoed my words to Rusty. She'd entered the arena. She must be the next to run. "I didn't know you barrel raced."

I looked up at her and smiled. "We've been practicing." Like that could explain what had just happened.

"For how long? Years?"

"Please exit the arena," the announcer droned, sounding even more annoyed than before – something I'd thought was impossible. Apparently, we hadn't impressed him as much as we had Kestrel.

I smiled at Kestrel. "Good luck! My fingers and toes are crossed for you."

"Sounds painful." She smiled back, but the tightness around her mouth told me she was already focusing on the race.

Rusty and I hurried out the gates and to a side rail. Kestrel was still standing in the starting position, her knuckles white as she gripped the reins, her face pale.

"Whenever you're ready," groaned the announcer.

Twitchy lunged forward. Moments later, they reached the first barrel and swept around it. I was impressed. Kestrel must have been practicing too. They were good, probably almost as good as Rusty on the turns. But no matter how hard she tried, poor old Twitchy just didn't have the speed anymore. Rusty and I had beaten her time, I was sure. So had the pinto. But had the pinto beaten Rusty? Or would someone else?

Kestrel rode her panting mare out of the ring, patting her on her shoulder and murmuring, "Good girl. Good girl."

"You did great!" I said when they stopped beside us.

Kestrel reached over and we high-fived. "Thanks. I think it's the best we've ever done. I don't even care that we lost."

"You don't know you lost," I said, thinking that maybe my run had just *seemed* super fast because I was riding.

Kestrel laughed. "I'd say that after being the third to run, Twitchy and I are now solidly in *third* place. For now anyway. Jake's about to go."

I glanced back at Wildfire. She was still in the corner, seemingly forgotten by everyone, thank goodness. She was looking nervously about – I could guess who for – and every few seconds her eyes rested on me.

He will find me, she said.

He does not know where you are.

I didn't have to ask who "he" was.

Applause interrupted my thoughts and I looked up to see Jake run his horse across the finish line, going about a hundred miles an hour. "How did he do?" I asked Kestrel.

She looked at me as if I was weird or something. "Weren't you watching?"

"I, uh, just got a little distracted."

"Hi, guys." Jon reined Coal in beside us, saving me from Kestrel's caustic comment and making my butterflies spin upward in aerial acrobatics.

"Hi," I said, brilliantly.

"Are you riding Coal in the Barrel Race?" Kestrel asked.

Jon shook his head. "I saw Evy and the girl on the pinto run. Coal wouldn't have a chance."

"Ha! So I do beat you!" Kestrel gloated.

"This time. Only this time. And that was awesome, Evy! You totally won it."

"No way." Equally brilliant comment. I was on a roll here.

We continued to chat for a bit, but because it's embarrassing, I'm not going to tell you any more of my stunning and extremely witty comments. Jon didn't seem the least bit tongue-tied – it almost made me think he didn't really like me. Either that, or it just wasn't fair. How come he could talk like a perfectly normal human and I always turned into a stuttering fool? But maybe he only *seemed* perfectly normal. I've only ever seen him when he's with me, and maybe his normal around me isn't really his *normal* normal, if you know what I mean.

He is coming. Wildfire's panic brushed through me and I turned to see her owner striding toward her, a dark scowl on his face. Without a word of explanation to Kestrel, who was talking to the dark-haired girl on the pinto anyway, I spun Rusty around and trotted toward Wildfire, arriving just as the man got there. The mare threw her ears back and her head snaked out. Only the reins, still wrapped around the rail, stopped her from biting him.

Do not hurt him, I implored.

Wildfire stamped her hoof and scowled at me.

"So are you buying her or not?" the man said, his face cross and his voice belligerent. "You have to make up your mind. I have other interested parties."

At first, I thought he was talking to me and was struck dumb by his brusqueness – but then Jon spoke behind me. "I'm not buying her." I hadn't even heard him ride after us. But no wonder – my heart was pounding like mad in my ears, I was so angry with this scummy guy. At least my negative thoughts were forcing the butterflies to take a break.

The man suddenly lunged forward and grabbed the mare's reins, just below the bit. She wasn't expecting it, so she didn't get to bite him. Then he shouldered closer to her and began to untie her, as her lips twitched, her teeth ground together.

"You drugged her!" I accused.

The man froze.

"And you tried to rip me off," Jon added, his voice shaking with barely suppressed rage.

This was true too, but the man didn't seem as concerned with Jon's claim. "It ain't my fault you can't ride, son," he said, a scornful smile twisting his mean face. "She was just feeling her oats a bit. I thought you said you knew how to handle a horse."

Okay, you can bite him, I told Wildfire and she did just that, jerking her reins from his hand and chomping down, swiftly and efficiently, on the man's upper arm. He cried out and jumped back, then raised his uninjured arm as if to strike Wildfire.

"Stay away from her!" I yelled, and in the face of his obvious brutality, I found my courage. "I bet you hit her all the time. No wonder she hates people."

The man glared at me as he clutched the growing bloody spot on his shirt.

"It's illegal to drug horses to make them act calm for sale, plus, it's cruelty to animals."

He blinked. I can't read human minds, but with this guy I didn't have to. Anyone could tell what he was thinking. He was desperate to get away from my accusations – and it made me wonder if he'd been charged with cruelty in the past.

"You've been charged with animal abuse before, haven't you," I said, making it sound like a statement, not a question.

"You don't know anything about me," he growled, stepping toward us. Rusty laid his ears back and stamped his front hoof. The man stopped short and glared at us.

"I know more than you think," I said, which wasn't a total bluff. I knew he'd been cruel to Wildfire. I knew that she both hated and feared him, and would do anything to escape him.

And then I heard my name droned in the announcer's voice. And clapping. And Kestrel cheering.

I'd won the Barrel Race.

"I'll buy her from you," I said, thinking it was now or never. He believed I knew he was an abuser, which put me in a position of power. "I'll give you fifty dollars."

The man's hand dropped to his side and he adopted a lax stance. Like he had all the time in the world. Like *he* was the one in control. Ha!

"Three hundred."

"You told me five hundred," Jon interjected, clearly still furious.

The man ignored Jon as he continued to lock eyes with me. "I'd get three hundred from the meat buyer," he said.

Ice jittered along my spine. I couldn't let Wildfire go to the meat buyer. "Seventy five."

"Two hundred."

Yes! He was willing to bargain. Which only meant he *was* afraid of what we'd say if he didn't sell Wildfire to us. Well, I could work with that!

Watching him out of the corner of my eye, I turned toward the spectators and riders standing around the arena. Unfortunately, there were no uniformed police officers in sight, and I couldn't see Charlie or either of Kestrel's parents – so I'd have to improvise. I waved to no one.

The man looked to see who I'd waved to, and the second he looked, I turned back to him and said, "One hundred dollars or I tell my friend over there about you drugging the horse."

He almost stepped back. "You can't prove anything."

"There will still be traces of it in her blood. All we need to do is ask the rodeo vet to take a sample. Plus after the way the mare freaked out in the arena, we have a lot of witnesses to her being dangerous."

The man narrowed his eyes and I narrowed mine right back. "One hundred fifty," he growled.

I shook my head. "One hundred, and you have five

more seconds to make up your mind." I couldn't believe I was pushing it so far, but there were the words, out of my mouth.

One.

Two.

I started to turn Rusty toward the crowd. Jon looked at me like I was nuts.

Three.

I asked Rusty to walk on.

Four.

"Okay, one hundred," the man said behind me. "In cash. Today."

Relief flowed through me like a river and I took a second to collect myself before I turned Rusty back to face the man. "Deal. Give me a few minutes to get the money, and I'll meet you back at your horse trailer. You can leave the mare here." I didn't want him hanging out with Wildfire while he waited. The mare hated him too much, and who knew what would happen if he stayed.

He reached out to shake my hand, and when I just looked at it like it was a gross bug, he snapped, "She's all yours. You two have fun," then turned and stalked off, anger oozing from him like fog. Wildfire kicked at him as he left, but thankfully, she missed by an inch.

"I can't believe I was going to buy her for five hundred," Jon said beside me, a hushed kind of respect in his voice. "But honestly, I think at one hundred, you got ripped off, Evy. And your mom's going to have a fit."

"If I'm lucky, Mom won't even meet her. I didn't buy her for a riding horse."

"Then why?"

I smiled. "I'm going to give her a gift."

"What do you mean?"

"Freedom. I'm giving her freedom, and hopefully it'll solve one of my problems at the same time."

The rest of the rodeo was a wonderful, heat-soaked, dusty, noisy, indulgent blur. After scowling at Wildfire's former owner as I paid him my hundred dollar prize money and got my bill of sale, I talked and laughed with dozens of different people until my cheeks felt like rubber from smiling so much. We watched the Downhill Mountain Race, breathless, as the horses and riders careened down the mountain in their headlong, hazardous dash to the finish line. I visited the talkative yearling again to give him a shoulder scratch, and Kestrel, Jon, and I ate heavenly gooey burgers, soggy fries, and sweet, greasy mini donuts until our stomachs churned in protest.

I tried giving some attention to Wildfire now and then, but other than accepting some food and water, she didn't want anything to do with me. I didn't blame her. I still hadn't given her what I promised. Instead, I was enjoying myself and making her wait. I knew I was going to set her free, but she had no idea if I'd keep my word or not. Considering that, plus how badly she hated humans, she was really quite civil to me.

Finally, three hours before sundown, Kestrel's mom told us to start back. I borrowed a halter and lead rope from Jon for Wildfire, said goodbye to all my new friends, and we started the long trek home. Jon and Caroline rode with us until the turn-off to their house, and a lot of other people were heading home as well. It wasn't until we were almost at Kestrel's ranch that we were finally alone.

It was weird – I'd been so happy to hear all the noise and excitement of the rodeo, but now the glorious silence sounded just as delightful. Not that it was a complete hush; there was the clip-clop of the horse's hooves on the hard packed dirt road, the birds warbling, the wind rustling the leaves, a distant cowbell, but these were all normal, everyday sounds. And then from behind us came the sound of a trotting horse.

I looked back to see a crimson-red horse and his rider catching up to us – Redwing and Charlie – while leading a bay and white pinto. Kestrel and I stopped to wait for them.

Charlie's eyes roamed over Wildfire as he approached us. "You didn't buy that crazy mare, did you, Evy?" he asked.

"I sure did," I said, sticking out my chin. "But she's not crazy, Charlie. She's just misunderstood."

Kestrel laughed beside me.

Charlie stopped Redwing and the pinto edged around him to sniff at Wildfire. "Well, if anyone can *speak* to her, you can."

Kestrel raised her eyebrows at this and I scowled at Charlie. Why did he have to hint about my gift in front of Kestrel? It's already a miracle that she's never guessed, and clues like that don't help.

"I'm going to let her go live with the wild stallion," I said quickly to change the topic. "I'm hoping he'll give up on Cocoa if he has a mare of his own."

Charlie laughed.

"What?" asked Kestrel. "Don't you think it will work?"

"Yes, I think so," said Charlie, his face lining around his grin. "I think it'll work so good that I had the same idea. I brought you this pinto to give to the mustang."

"Really?" What awesome news. Surely, he'd leave Cocoa alone if he had *two* mares to take care of and protect. "How did you get her?"

"She's a donation. Her owner said she gets lame if she's worked hard a couple days in a row. He needs a horse that he can take out on week-long hunting trips, so he has no use for her."

"Will she be okay out in the bush?"

"She'll be fine. She won't be packing gear thirty or forty miles a day out there."

"She's cute. What's her name?" asked Kestrel, leaning down to stroke the intelligent, blazed face.

"He didn't say."

I breathed a sigh of relief. At least Charlie didn't tell Kestrel to ask *me* for her name. However, I could do just that. And I would, as soon as there were no humans around to notice if I acted distracted.

"We better get going. I have to be home before dark." I reached for the pinto's lead rope.

"You don't mind finding the stallion?" he asked, handing her over.

I shook my head. "Not even a little bit. Stop by the next time you're out our way to get the halter and lead rope."

He nodded. "See you soon, then." He turned Redwing away and started back toward town. They were loping before he turned the corner, obviously in a hurry to get back.

"I can take her," Kestrel said, holding out her hand. I passed the pinto's lead rope over, and we were off.

The pinto really was a sweetie. She seemed bright and perky, and wasn't obstinate about being led, like Wildfire. No pulling back or racing ahead for her. And her emotions were lovely to sense. She had a bright way of looking at life, as if she completely believed that everything was going to turn out for the best. And maybe it would for her. Things have a way of working out for those who think it will, at least eventually. I couldn't help but hope that her upbeat attitude would help poor Wildfire feel better about life too. The chestnut mare still looked awfully fearful and depressed, even though her previous owner no longer had control over her.

It was already mid-evening when we reached Kestrel's, but we had to stop. Since her parents and sisters weren't home yet, Kestrel left a note on the kitchen table saying she was going to my house to help me and would be home the next afternoon. Then she grabbed a letter from the counter, some cookies from the jar, and we were off again.

"A reply from Ally," she said, waving the envelope in the air as we left the house. "I forgot to tell you this morning."

"Wow, that's fast. Maybe she has some news for us."

"Do you want to read it now?" she asked, as we mounted our horses.

"Let's wait. Mom will never let me out again if I don't get home in time." Plus, I needed to scan for the wild stallion. If the letter held interesting news about my mom or Edward, I'd have a lot harder time concentrating on mustangs.

Even as Kestrel and I kept up a perma-chatter, I kept my horse senses wide open, hoping to pick up the wild stallion. I preferred to turn Wildfire and the pinto loose before we got home because then there wouldn't be so many questions, but there wasn't a peep from him as we rode along. Could he have given up on stealing Cocoa and left our area to start his herd elsewhere? If so, what was I going to do with these two horses? Mom wouldn't be super thrilled to have two more dependents, one recurringly lame and another who hated people.

More than once, as we talked and rode through the dying light, I was struck by how much I was going to miss Kestrel when she went to school. My life was going to nosedive when she left, and now that the rodeo was over that nosedive loomed just on the horizon.

"I love the sunset," said Kestrel, when we finished talking about her conversation with the girl who owned the fleet-footed pinto.

I turned. The sky was awesome – and then it turned from awesome to stunningly amazing. The slanting sunrays sparked the clouds, turning them to flame: red and vermillion and crimson and cherry. The light smoldered so bright that everything around us glowed. Rusty looked pink and Twitchy was dark maroon, while the trees and grasses and bushes all claimed varying radiant shades between.

How much time would pass before we rode through another amazing sunset together? Beside me, Kestrel sighed contentedly. I copied her, but my sigh sounded more dissatisfied than anything. If only she'd tell me she wasn't going away to school. If only she'd change her mind. But I knew that was one thing she *would* tell me as soon as she decided, *if* she decided to stay. She'd only delay telling me the truth if she'd already decided to go – and since she hadn't said anything yet, I could only hope she hadn't decided yet.

Mom was waiting for us on the porch when we rode around the last corner. As soon as she saw us, she slumped a little – relieved, I guess. She'd told me to get home at sunset and the sunset was fading already. She hurried down the porch steps, then walked briskly

to greet us, her arms wrapped around her middle and Loonie at her heels.

"I hope she doesn't mind that I came for the night," Kestrel said, her dark hair glowing with the last of the sunset's red.

"She'll be glad. She loves it when you come. She might not be too glad to see Wildfire and the pinto, though."

Kestrel looked at me. "I didn't know you named her."

"It just seemed to suit her."

"It *really* suits her. She's red chestnut, has a fiery personality, and was a little out of control today. Sounds like a wildfire to me."

I laughed. "That's totally her. But let's keep the out-of-control thing to ourselves, okay?"

"I'll let you do all the explaining," Kestrel said.

And then Mom reached us. "I'm so glad to see you, Evy." She put her hand on my knee and gazed up into my face with reddened eyes – and the red wasn't a sunset reflection. She'd been crying.

"We're not late, Mom, and I was perfectly safe today."

Her face contorted as she tried to rein her emotions in enough to speak. "I'm so sorry."

"Why? What for?" I didn't get what the big deal was. So I'd gone to a rodeo, and then I'd come home. Nothing else had happened. Except, oh yeah, bringing home two new horses. But Wildfire and the pinto couldn't be causing this extreme reaction, could they? Maybe it was our fight. Guilt spiked me in the heart. I *had* been awfully mean to her.

"The horse…"

"I'm not planning to keep them, I promise," I said with relief. So it *was* the two extra horses that were upsetting her. "They're here for just a day or so."

Mom looked confused for a moment, then shook her head. "No, no."

"It's something else. Something's wrong," Kestrel said quietly beside me.

Mom nodded, then her tear-filled eyes caught mine again. "This morning, I took my time coming back. I did some sketches and didn't get home until early afternoon."

"Yeah?" I said, still not understanding. What was so terrible about her stopping to sketch?

"While I was gone, that horse, the wild one, he came here." Emotion threatened to stop her voice again.

And then a horrible thought shot into my mind. Twilight. But she'd been in her stall when we left that morning. She'd been protected. The wild stallion wouldn't have gone into the barn. He couldn't have opened her stall door.

Immediately, I reached out to touch her mind. She had to be here, she just had to be here.

But she wasn't.

"I took so long that Twilight must've fiddled with the catch on her stall door until she opened it. She was free when he arrived," Mom said. "And he took her. And I'm so sorry, Evy. So sorry."

There was nothing we could do that night. Mom showed me where Twilight's hoof prints met the stallion's and there was no mistaking that they'd left together. I felt awful, shuddery and sick, all the time we cared for the horses and Tumpoo.

Mom helped us with Rusty and Twitchy so that Kestrel and I could get the two new mares settled. She asked us questions about the rodeo all the while – I think to distract us, because she didn't seem too interested in our answers. The only thing that sparked a bit of concern in her was when she went to stroke Wildfire's shoulder and the mare jumped away. I had to explain that Wildfire didn't really like people, and Mom avoided her after that.

Mom really seemed to like the little pinto, though. I must admit, I did too, and Kestrel was madly in love. We further diverted our worries for Twilight by going through names for the sweet-natured mare. At one point, I took a chance on being caught and reached out to touch her mind. The pinto thought of herself as Cricket, and when I mentioned the name, both Kestrel and Mom laughed. Kestrel thought it was perfect, while Mom thought I'd mentioned it as a joke. She said she was going to call the mare Cupcake, and in the end, we called the pinto Cricket Cupcake – a weird combination I know, but even more strangely, the name seemed to suit her.

After we got the horses settled, Mom went back to the house and Kestrel and I decided to hang out with Tumpoo for a while. He was acting all glum and sorry for himself, giving us pitiful, forlorn glances, and clearly feeling neglected after being left alone for most of the day.

We made a plan for morning as we hung out in his stall. We'd leave early, at first light, and follow their trail while bringing the two mares with us. Hopefully they'd not only attract the wild stallion, but also distract him enough that he'd stop guarding Twilight – which would be our chance to get her away from him.

And if we didn't find his trail? If we couldn't distract him with the mares? I had no idea. Hopefully, we could solve those problems if they appeared.

When our meager plans were made, we sat down and leaned against the back wall. Tumpoo settled in the straw beside us within easy petting reach, and Kestrel opened Ally's letter – and *tried* to read it aloud. Tried, because Tumpoo couldn't have us focusing on anything other than him and kept trying to grab the paper in his wiggly brown lips. When Kestrel jumped up to pace and read, the weanling jumped up right behind her.

"We went to the gallery that you told me about and looked for your mom's paintings," Kestrel read aloud after reading a whole page about Ally's new kitten. "They are *soooo* much money! My dad thought I had good taste when I said they were my favorites, but that he'd *never* be able to buy one for me. And they really are my favorites. They're gorgeous! I especially liked the one called Ice Dances. That one was the most expensive too, though."

Kestrel jumped back as Tumpoo made a particularly clever feint for the letter and barely missed. She shoved the letter into my hand and then grabbed the moose around the neck. "So you want to wrestle, you big brat?"

While Kestrel was being flung about, I continued to read aloud. "The guy who was selling them said that the paintings were going fast and that he just got Ice Dances. He said that if we wanted it, we needed to buy it soon or it would be gone. My dad said we'd buy it *after* we won the lottery, and the guy looked kind of mad. I think he hoped we were rich." I grinned. I could just imagine Edward's face. He'd be furious about a snarky comment like that, especially if he first thought he was going to make a big sale.

I continued reading but there was nothing more about my mom's paintings. Ally sure had a weird family, though – but I guess she could say the same thing about me with my hermit mom and my horses, dog, cats, and

moose, not to mention the adventures that Kestrel and I
have with our horses.

"That doesn't really tell us much," I said, standing up
and pushing the letter into my pocket. "Edward would
tell Ally and her dad that the paintings are selling fast,
even if it wasn't true, just to push them into buying one."

"It tells us that the paintings are expensive, though,"
said Kestrel, holding Tumpoo in a tight headlock.

"Maybe he's asking too much money. Maybe that's
why they aren't selling very well. Maybe that three-day-
eventer could afford one because she's rich."

"I wish Ally had told us how many paintings there
were in the gallery. Then we'd know how many were
selling."

I could feel a big headache starting. There was
still too little information and far too many mountains
of stuff to worry about: with this mystery, Kestrel
potentially leaving, and most of all, Twilight being
stolen. "Let's not think about it now," I said. "We have
to get to sleep."

We slid out of Tumpoo's stall and patted him
goodnight. He bawled after us as we left the barn,
sounding like he was at the apex of misery. He'd really
missed us today, the poor guy. But we had to go to bed;
we'd be getting up when it was still dark outside and
leaving as soon as the sky lightened in the east. His
piteous bleating followed us all the way to the cabin,
as if he already knew he was going to have another
long day in his stall tomorrow while Kestrel and I were

out searching for Twilight. I really had to figure out a long term solution for him. He didn't deserve all this captivity.

It was torture trying to get to sleep while thinking about Twilight being stolen away. I couldn't help but try to sense her constantly and kept thinking I heard her when I was almost asleep. Most of the time it was a stray thought from one of the new mares and sometimes it was simply my imagination, but the result was the same. More staring into the dark and listening to Kestrel snore. But I did get to sleep. Finally.

I thought I'd be exhausted the next morning, but my eyes seemed to open of their own will, five minutes before the alarm clock went off. I lit the kerosene lamp, which woke Kestrel, and the two of us got dressed in layers. It was going to be cold in the early morning, and then a lot warmer later during the day. We needed to be prepared for both.

Mom was in the kitchen, her face all puffy with sleep. She was dishing up steaming bowls of porridge for us, which we gratefully consumed after a quick trip to the barn to give the horses and Tumpoo their breakfasts. I didn't feel that hungry – it was way too early for that – but I knew I'd really appreciate it later when I had energy and wasn't so hungry that all I could think about was my screaming stomach.

"I want you girls to be home by suppertime," Mom said as we pulled our riding boots on by the door.

I opened my mouth to protest, but Mom's words beat

me to it. "Yes, even if you haven't found Twilight yet. Kestrel is supposed to be home today. That'll give her enough time to get there before dark."

I didn't argue. There was no point. I didn't know if I could force myself to stop the hunt if we hadn't found Twilight yet, but maybe we'd locate her quickly. That would be the best – then I wouldn't have to find out if I would blatantly disobey Mom.

We saddled Rusty and Twitchy, shoved our lunches in our saddlebags, haltered Cricket Cupcake and Wildfire, and were off. Tumpoo's mournful calls followed us as we rode away from the cabin. And so did Loonie. I sent her back with a firm command. She slunk back to the house, making me feel like the meanest person alive, but I couldn't let her come with us. We were on a mustang hunt and she was a dog. She'd bark, making the wild stallion run, and he'd force Twilight to run before him.

We rode to the tracks Mom had shown us the evening before and tried to follow them, but they disappeared just a few feet on. I turned Rusty in the direction the stallion trotted on the first day I saw him; he may have come and gone by the same route. Great thinking, but unfortunately, nothing but pine needles, forest plants, dead branches, and no tracks lay beneath the trees. Kestrel and I split up, she with Cricket Cupcake and I with Wildfire, and we rode a massive circle through the woods and around the pasture, cabin, and little lake.

It wasn't until I reached the lake that I saw the horse tracks. He'd come from behind the house this time, and he and Twilight had left the same way. Kestrel, Twitchy, and Cricket Cupcake burst from the trees across the lake – and almost scared Wildfire to death. She lunged away, jerking my saddle and Rusty's poor back.

Nothing to fear. Nothing to hurt you, I reassured her while clinging to Rusty's mane. Her panic thudded into me as she strained away from us, the sensation mixing with Rusty's pain.

Hurting Rusty, I told her. *Stop pulling.*

This time she listened. Her fear ebbed a little, and then, when still nothing had attacked her, she calmed a bit more. She was going to make a great wild horse, startling at the slightest movement. When Kestrel, Twitchy, and Cricket Cupcake drew near, I pointed out the tracks to Kestrel.

"Good thing they went close to the lake," said Kestrel.

I agreed. If it wasn't for the mud, we probably wouldn't have found the tracks. We didn't waste any time; I kept my horse radar on high as we trotted alongside the lake and then into the forest, alternately glancing down at the ground, where it was now too dry to show tracks, and straight ahead, where I hoped to recognize something that would be appealing to a mustang, like a meadow, a dusty place to roll, a salt lick…

Suddenly, to my right, I spotted a grassy clearing. They would have made the detour, I was sure.

Yes! There at the edge of the meadow, neat little hoof prints; Twilight had walked here.

Predator!

Wildfire's fear impaled me as Rusty and I were jerked sideways again.

Stop it!

Wildfire froze. I took a moment to collect the remnants of my thoughts – it was a struggle even to remember who I was for a second – and then felt terrible. I'd mind-yelled at her, the poor thing. She couldn't help being afraid. *Sorry.*

Wildfire snorted.

Rusty scowled at her.

"What was that all about?" asked Kestrel.

"I don't know."

And then I heard him – and I knew why Wildfire had spooked. Kestrel and I groaned in unison. The brown furry form hurried out of the bushes, whimpering with happiness at finding us. Tumpoo. He had somehow freed himself and followed us.

The first thing he did was crowd up to Rusty, which of course sent Wildfire into another tizzy. She'd never been so close to a moose before, even a small one, and she'd already decided she didn't like it. Cricket Cupcake, on the other hand, simply found the moose calf interesting. She pulled forward to sniff at him while Wildfire pulled away. Rusty and Twitchy merely wondered what all the fuss was about.

"Do you want to take him back?"

I shook my head. "It would take too long. We wouldn't get back here until almost noon, and then we'd only have three hours left to search before we'd have to start back."

Kestrel pulled on Cricket Cupcake's lead rope, making her move behind Twitchy again, then asked the old mare to walk on. The moose followed them, and Rusty and I pulled Wildfire after the calf. At first she tugged, stiff-legged, against the rope, but then seemed to realize how silly she was being and started walking like a normal horse.

"How are we going to control him if we see Twilight?" asked Kestrel. "You know how clumsy he is. He might just bumble ahead and scare the wild stallion."

"I know. He'll probably see Twilight and make a run for her, thinking it's time to play." I couldn't keep the depression from my voice. Tumpoo ruined everything. And yet how could I be mad at him? He looked so happy, cavorting along with all his horsey friends, both old and new; he was so naïve, he even thought Wildfire liked him. Rejection was a foreign concept to him. And he was so obviously pleased with himself for finding us.

What was I going to do with him if we found Twilight and the wild stallion? He didn't stay on command, I couldn't talk to him, and we certainly couldn't tie him up. He'd start to bawl and attract every meat-eater within hearing range. But we couldn't afford to lose a half day of searching, either – so there was nothing else for it but to keep going and hope for the best.

After the soft spot in the meadow, we saw no sign of tracks again. We made intelligent horse guesses and

I asked Rusty when I wasn't sure which would be the best way to go. And then, about two hours later, we came across fresh horse poop. Stallion poop. I could tell because he'd gone on top of an old pile. It's a trick that wild stallions use to frighten away rival stallions. The rival is supposed to come along and see the massive poo and think, "I don't want to fight that guy. He's huge!" And then run away.

After Tumpoo bumbled over the pile of poo, knocking it to half its height, we continued on. Kestrel and I and the horses walked sedately in single file and Tumpoo was with us one moment and gone the next, off on little trips of exploration. I was just thinking that we were getting close – I could almost feel a Twilight-ness in the air – when I heard her. I stiffened on Rusty's back and strained to listen. She was barely coming into range. I closed my eyes to concentrate better and allowed Rusty to follow Twitchy and Cricket Cupcake unguided.

Yes, I could hear her more clearly now and – I felt sick – Twilight was having fun? A delightful coolness spread across my stomach and I realized she was splashing herself in a small creek, enjoying the sun on her back and the cold wetness on her stomach. Not a single, tiny, miniscule concern marred the landscape of her mind. How could she not be worried?

A horrible thought nagged me and I pushed it away. It nagged louder. I gave it a huge shove. It came right back, yelling.

Had Twilight gone with the stallion willingly?

Maybe she'd had enough of domestic life and decided to return to the wild. I felt like opening my mouth and howling with sadness even at the possibility of it being true.

Did Twilight *want* to leave me?

Helpless to stop my thoughts, they turned to all the times I'd acted impatient with her the last few weeks, the times I'd yelled instead of scolding gently. The times I'd let my frustrations rule my actions.

"Evy? Are you okay?" Trust Kestrel to notice the guilt and misery that must be splayed all over my face.

For a moment, I couldn't speak. And then the words came in a rush. "What if Twilight doesn't want to come home? What if she wants to be wild again? What if she wants to stay with the mustang stallion and be part of his herd?"

"She wants to come home."

"But how can you be sure? How can you know that?"

"She loves you."

"What if…" The whisper scraped from my throat. "What if she doesn't love me enough?"

Kestrel was silent for a moment, then she sighed. "She'll always love you, Evy. But if she decides to go back to the wild anyway, well, you'll be okay."

I shuddered. *Not* what I wanted to hear. I wanted to hear that I was being ridiculous to even consider the notion that Twilight would ever leave me. I wanted to hear that there was no way she'd ever go back to being a wild horse. That she'd *never* choose the wild stallion over me. I wanted to hear anything but what Kestrel had actually said.

But, miserably, I knew she was right. I would survive – barely. And Twilight would be okay too. She'd probably miss me for a while, but she'd be doing what she wanted to do and would feel happy. And neither of us would ever forget the time we'd lived together.

"Yeah, but that won't make it any easier to say goodbye." What I couldn't say out loud was that I'd feel like my heart was being ripped from my chest when Twilight left. *If* Twilight left, I reminded myself. Maybe this was all just a nightmare fantasy and she had no intention of leaving me.

"But really, I think she loves you and Rusty and living in your family. I don't think she'll go wild again. She's even getting to like Tumpoo."

I smiled at Kestrel – a weak, wan smile, but still a smile – and for the first time in ages I felt glad she never told me things just to make me feel better. "Yeah, too much. They've become partners in crime."

"So… you're okay?"

I nodded.

"So where do we go now?"

I gathered my sadness in a tight little bundle, wishing

all the while that my own emotions could be shut away like the horses, and reached over it with my horse-sense. Twilight was still enjoying the coolness of the creek and she was ahead and to our left. And this time I noticed something else too, something that now clouded the perfection of the moment for her. Irritation. Not just plain irritation, but sudden and supreme annoyance. The stallion was now standing on the bank, watching her, and just knowing he was there made her angry. I felt her turn her back to him and continue splashing. I smiled. No one could ignore someone quite like Twilight could. She was a master at it. That stallion was going to feel so slighted that I almost felt sorry for him. Almost.

Twilight, we are here to bring you home.

Finally! I felt her stop splashing and throw her head up, looking for us.

Wait until I say before you come to us. I have a plan.

What plan?

Cannot talk now. Kestrel here.

Grudging acceptance from Twilight. She would've liked veto power over our plan, I think. But there was no time to explain. Not only was it too hard to talk to both Twilight and Kestrel at once, but Tumpoo was still off on one of his adventures. If we could get Wildfire and Cricket Cupcake turned loose, plus Twilight saved, *before* the moose calf jumped out from behind a bush, bleating, spastically cavorting about, and scaring the pants off all the horses, things would go sooo much more smoothly.

"Let's go this direction," I said, as innocently as possible to Kestrel, and reined Rusty slightly to the left. Twitchy followed automatically and Cricket Cupcake crowded right on her heels. She obviously didn't like being the last in line.

We walked for about three minutes, talking a bit as we rode, and then I told Kestrel that I thought I heard something.

"I heard it too, a minute ago," she said. "I think Tumpoo is behind us."

A twig snapped back in the woods and visions of leaping cougars and charging bears lurched into my head. If only it was one of them rather than Tumpoo. Just kidding!

"Let's hurry," I said. "What I heard was ahead of us. Splashing. It could be Twilight. She loves splashing herself in water on hot days like today."

Keep splashing, I told Twilight, thinking that Kestrel might hear it soon, plus the sound of our approach might be somewhat masked.

"Awesome," Kestrel whispered. "Let's go."

So we went. Closer and closer. Behind us, the crunching forest floor crunched louder. Wildfire kept looking back, the whites of her eyes flashing in the shadows. One extra loud snap and she lunged forward. Only the strong lead rope, snubbed to Rusty's saddle horn, kept her from racing away. My telling her it was probably just Tumpoo didn't make her feel any safer. Not that she thought I was purposefully lying to her –

she hadn't decided yet whether I was a truth-teller or not. She just thought I was basically clueless, like all the other ignorant humans.

With Wildfire lunging on the rope, Rusty trying to bite her every time she tried passing him, Twitchy lagging behind, Cricket Cupcake trying hard not to be the last in line, and Tumpoo sounding like a full-grown bull moose crashing along behind us, we came to a narrow strip of meadow nestled in the trees.

I stopped Rusty and turned to Kestrel. "This is perfect," I whispered to her. "We just need to get Twilight to come running and then turn the mares loose when she and the stallion are halfway down the meadow. That way, he'll see these two before he sees us and panics."

"But how are you going to call her? Won't he take off if he hears a human yelling, just like last time?"

Drat my loud mouth. "Um, good point." What else could I say?

Twilight, run toward us. Now!

There is no word to describe Twilight in that moment, other than *glee*. It glowed from every particle of her being as she sprang toward us, leapt up the creek bank, bit the surprised stallion as she ripped past him, then let her rear hooves fly in his face to give herself another precious second's lead. He was faster than she was, and she knew it. However, both she and I knew that she was smarter and obviously far, *far* sassier.

"Which way should we go?" I asked to give Twilight time to reach us.

Kestrel's forehead wrinkled as she thought. She looked up the skinny meadow and then down it.

Tumpoo crackled closer to us.

Wildfire lunged forward again, and this time, Rusty was seriously mad at her. Every time she didn't think before she leapt, his back wrenched with pain. I hauled on the lead rope, hoping to pull Wildfire closer to us and get some of the sideways pressure off the saddle.

"I don't believe it," Kestrel breathed beside me.

I looked up, expecting to see Twilight, and saw a gold and black streak racing from the far end of the meadow. I'd never seen her run so fast. Her legs were a blur and her body almost seemed to be touching the ground, she was so low. Right behind her – totally focused on her and not us – ran the palomino stallion.

"Untie Cricket," I gasped, and pulled Wildfire even closer.

Hold still, Rusty. Do not bite her.

I clutched the cheek strap of Wildfire's halter as I undid the buckle with my other hand, and then the halter broke away and she was free. Rusty immediately connected with a well placed nip on her shoulder, which sent Wildfire trotting into the meadow and looking back at him with a hurt expression on her face. Cricket Cupcake followed Wildfire, they sniffed noses, and then they noticed Twilight and the wild stallion running toward them.

They trotted away.

I couldn't believe it, especially of Wildfire. All she'd

ever wanted was to be free. How did she think wild horses lived? Alone, as solitary creatures? No, they lived in herds. And surely she could see that this handsome young fellow was the perfect match for her. Not only was he strong and beautiful but he'd protect her from carnivores and other threats, plus he was actively seeking a family. What more could she ask for?

I waved my arm in the air, hoping to get them to run toward Twilight and the mustang, but they didn't even look at me – so Rusty lunged after them. Thank goodness I was holding his mane with my other hand.

The mares scattered and Rusty took off after Cricket Cupcake, probably thinking she was the less stubborn of the two. She ran in a wide arc toward the center of the meadow, and as Rusty galloped after her, I ducked over his neck. I didn't want the stallion to notice me and be frightened off – though the chances of that looked bizarrely low. He still seemed utterly focused on Twilight.

And he was closer to her.

And he was gaining on her.

Rusty and I got Cricket Cupcake moving toward the racing pair and then Twilight was past us, her head straight out, her mane and tail whipping behind her. Great gasps came from her mouth. Clearly, this wasn't fun anymore. She was desperate to get away.

Then the stallion raced past Cricket Cupcake, Rusty, and me. All three of us turned and looked after him in astonishment. Hadn't he seen the beautiful, gracious, and sweet-tempered Cricket Cupcake?

Now Twilight was turning in a large circle and heading for Wildfire. The chestnut galloped faster for a moment, then *finally* seemed to understand what was happening. She screeched to a halt and, with her head held high, neighed to the stallion.

He didn't even falter. I couldn't believe his concentration. It was like we were all invisible. I couldn't help but think about the first time he'd tried to steal Twilight. Then, just the sound of our voices had frightened him off – but that was before Twilight was *his*. Now that he had her, he wasn't about to give her up.

Twilight whipped past Wildfire, not daring to slow down, and it was a good thing she didn't, because the stallion didn't either – not even when Wildfire reached out and greeted him as he streaked past.

Help me!

Run toward Rusty.

I straightened on Rusty's back and asked him to gallop back to the meadow's edge. Cricket Cupcake and Wildfire were on their own now, new mustangs. If I could break the stallion's fixation on Twilight, I knew Wildfire, at least, would be glad to approach him.

Kestrel rode Twitchy to meet me and together we turned to face Twilight and the stallion.

Run between us, I told Twilight.

She headed straight for the gap, about six feet wide, and shot through like a cannonball.

And the stallion stopped. He reared in front of us, so stunning and unruly and magnificent that my throat ached – and then he dashed around Rusty and kept after Twilight.

I spun Rusty around, ready to chase that stallion until the day I died. He wasn't forcing my Twilight away from me if I could do *anything* about it.

"Oh. My. Gosh," Kestrel said beside me.

My sentiments exactly.

The stallion was no longer chasing Twilight. In fact, he was screeching to an undignified and gangly stop. I took immediate advantage, urging Rusty forward and yelling. Kestrel and Twitchy were right beside us, Kestrel screaming like a banshee. The poor stallion jumped forward, then sideways when Tumpoo's sharp cloven hooves struck out at him – then he turned tail and ran, his white tail clamped tight to his hindquarters as he looked back over his shoulder, wild-eyed.

A loud choking giggle escaped Kestrel. I couldn't stop laughing either as I watched the stallion's ignoble retreat and then looked back at Twilight's gallant defender. Tumpoo had never looked so grumpy in all the months I'd known him. Rusty stepped back as the hefty calf snorted and then struck the ground with his sharp front hooves in a quick triple strike.

Only Twilight seemed unconcerned. She stood behind him, breathing heavily, somehow looking even more smug than usual as she watched the stallion give up and gallop off to meet his new family.

"You're the hero, Tumpoo," said Kestrel, and the

moose shook his head. His floppy ears made a thwacking sound as they hit the sides of his face.

"Yes, you are," I said, "Don't deny it." Even though I knew he wasn't denying anything. I got off of Rusty and walked toward Tumpoo, then thought better of it and decided to wait for the irritated look to fade just a bit more.

Instead I walked well around him to Twilight. *I am sorry,* I said, touching her lathered neck.

Why sorry?

For not being home to help you.

Not your fault.

I am still sorry.

Silly. Twilight nosed my hand.

Are you okay? I asked.

Okay.

I slipped my arm around her golden neck, not caring that her sweat was soaking into my shirt. She was safe, no thanks to me. But still, she seemed fine after her unwelcome adventure, and that was all that really mattered.

"They look nice together."

I looked up at Kestrel. She was watching the mustangs. And she was right. The horses – red, gold, and dark-spotted – looked lovely together, like they belonged, or something. And bonus, they were getting along. Cricket Cupcake was apparently going to be the boss mare, even though Wildfire was bigger. While Wildfire cuddled up to the love of her life, Cricket

Cupcake was actually telling them it was time to go. And they listened to her.

As the pinto mare led the way across the meadow, Wildfire fell in behind her and the stallion trailed love-struck in the rear.

Grateful.

I breathed deeply with satisfaction. *Thank you, Wildfire.* I sent warm feelings toward Cricket Cupcake and even though I didn't mind-speak to her, I felt a delicious fuzzy feeling flow back.

The three walked into the forest at the far side of the meadow, then the branches closed around them, waved, and were still. Kestrel sighed beside me. "I hope we see them again."

"Me too." Twilight bumped my knee. She didn't need to say anything. I knew what she wanted. Oats. "We should start back."

"Yeah."

The ride home was amazingly fast. I thought we'd be held back by Tumpoo and Twilight, but no such thing happened. They goofed off, bounced around, and sniffed at everything interesting within a hundred yard radius, but kept moving forward at a steady pace as if they were in a hurry to get home too.

We arrived just in time for supper. The horses had a quick bite of oats as Kestrel and I gulped down our food and told Mom about Twilight's rescue. For the first time in ages, Mom laughed. It was so nice to hear, like the trill of birds after a long, frigid winter.

Then it was time to ride Kestrel halfway home. We got on our horses, rounded up our animal entourage, and took off again. Loonie watched us go with melancholy eyes – until I called her, and then she frolicked after us like an ungainly, arthritic puppy. Mom stood on the porch and watched us go. She waved to me when I looked back, just before rounding the corner.

"So what are we going to do about Ally's letter?" Kestrel asked, as soon as we were out of sight of the cabin. "You should write back and ask for more help."

"Yeah, I was thinking about that, but I'm not sure what to ask her. She already went to his art gallery."

"What if we asked her to do an internet search on Edward?"

"But what could we learn from that?"

"I don't know. Maybe he charges too much for *all* the paintings he sells, and not just your mom's. Or hey, what if Laticia's paintings *are* selling?"

I opened my eyes wide at this. "You mean he might be selling them and keeping the money for himself?" The thought was new and terrible. Could he be that cold when he knew how much that money meant to us? We were struggling just to make ends meet. We ate a *lot* of rice and wore jeans, fleeces, and t-shirts, and grew our own vegetables. "I don't think he'd do that. It's stealing."

Kestrel shrugged. "It's too bad that Ally didn't see how many of Laticia's paintings were in the gallery. If we knew how many there were, you would know how many had sold, right?"

"Unless he puts them in storage after a while."

"Maybe she could ask to see *all* the paintings by that artist."

"Great idea, except he's already seen her and probably remembers her dad's lottery comment," I said, glumly. But there was still one way to find out. One more person we could send to Edward's gallery – and though I hated to even think about this horrible topic, I somehow forced myself to choke out the words. "What if you went in there, when you go away to school?"

A song sparrow warbled in the evening air, and the clop of the horse's hooves swelled around us as I fought to control my tears.

"You know, Evy, I've been thinking," Kestrel said, finally. "Today, what we did, that was amazing."

"Yeah, it really was," I whispered, knowing exactly what she meant. "How many people get to help start a wild horse herd?"

"I know. It can't get any cooler."

So she was changing the subject. She couldn't bring herself to tell me that she was going away. "I wonder if there will be any foals next year," I squeaked out, trying to play along. Maybe it would be easier that way, for both of us.

"I hope so."

Kestrel sighed. Loonie panted happily beside me, then the sound of her breathing was gone. I turned my head to see her sniffing a bush, an ecstatic look on her canine face. I didn't want to know what she smelled.

To make her look that happy, it had to be something thoroughly disgusting.

"How can I leave all this?"

My breath stopped short.

"I'd always be wondering what adventure you were off on or what mischief Twilight and Tumpoo were up to. If I'd gone to boarding school last year, I would've missed out on tracking the wolf and finding her puppies. I wouldn't have been here to help save Tumpoo when he was just hours old. I would have missed out on the crazy adventures with the poachers. Well, I *did* miss out on that, but I was here when you got home and I was the first one to hear what happened. And it all would have been for what?"

"For malls and movies and concerts and parks and well, *normal* things," I said.

"I have the rest of my life for normal stuff, after I grow up and leave home." Kestrel drew in a deep breath of evening scented air. "It's not worth it. Wilderness adventures and wild things, or a mall and movie once in a while." She laughed a short laugh like a bark. "It seems kind of silly now, to want that."

"So you're not going?" I said, every word falling like a weight from my mouth.

"I'm staying," Kestrel said firmly, and grinned over at me. "You're not getting off the hook as my best friend for a long, long time."

"Not ever, I hope," I said, smiling back.

"Not ever," Kestrel confirmed.

Lightness filled me from my toes to the tips of my ears. Kestrel was staying! She'd chosen me and the wilderness over movies and tons of normal friends and shopping and an education taught by teachers that you saw every day. I couldn't stop smiling, even as we reached the halfway point and we said goodbye. But Kestrel understood why I was grinning like a fool. She just grinned back, waved goodbye, then asked Twitchy to trot on.

I watched her ride away and waited... and as I thought she would, she turned at the corner and waved once more. I waved back, my goofy smile still plastered to my face. Then she was gone.

I patted Rusty on the shoulder.

She is not going away.

Good, said Rusty.

Twilight snorted her approval and bunted Tumpoo with her head, pushing him toward home. It was time to head back.

The evening sky was turning red again and this sunset promised to be as dazzling as the last. Twilight and Tumpoo started playing a chasing game in front of us, as Rusty walked serenely along.

"What goofs," I said and Loonie looked up at me, a big doggy grin on her face. She loved coming with us so much – and I loved her to come.

My smile slipped from my face. Now that the excitement of the rodeo was over and Kestrel was staying, I needed to take care of some important stuff.

First, Loonie's days of running beside us were ending. I needed to face it. She was not only half blind, but going deaf. She was arthritic and old, and one day, she would die. And there was only one thing I could do about it: spend lots and lots of time with her while I still could.

Second, I needed to apologize to Mom. She'd been right when she said I didn't really want to leave our wilderness home but I'd been too proud to admit it.

Third, I had to glean a *lot* more information if I was ever going to solve the mysteries surrounding my mom – not only her past now, but also the stuff with Edward and her paintings. Was he really stealing from us, as Kestrel guessed? For all of my life, we'd trusted him. He wouldn't betray that trust. Would he?

And finally, there was Tumpoo. I needed to get him behaving more like a moose and less like a horse. Somehow. Hmmm…

I lay down on Rusty's mane and Loonie darted around the other side of us so she could watch my face. Her fur glowed pink in the sunset, making her look like a dog angel. Twilight trotted up to walk beside Loonie, then Tumpoo pushed in between them, stretching his step so he could match strides with the horses.

My friends, my wonderful, fantastic friends. How lucky I was to belong to them. With them beside me, I could conquer anything. And then it was back – the silly grin. Somehow it found its way to my face again.